Whispers Under the Chestnut

Susan Lavin and Patti Sapp

ISBN: 9781735476896

Cover design by: Susan Lavin

Contents

Namaste

As Casey arrived at Amanda's farm early in the evening she was greeted by Norman, one of her favorite baby goats. He gently head-butted her hip and gave her an affectionate nuzzle.

"Well, hello there. Are you looking for attention?" Casey inquired. The black and white furry fellow replied with a funny burp-like, "Erpkk!"

Casey already knew this was going to be an interesting experience. It was almost summer, her favorite time of year. She was dressed in a loose green cotton shirt and black yoga shorts with her wavy auburn hair pulled up in a topknot. Amanda greeted her, looking amused, "Thanks for coming early. I could use a hand rounding up our playful friends."

Amanda, and her husband, Tony, owned

Chestnut Farm, which included a variety of gardens, chicken coops, and many shelters for the other animals. They were content in their cozy farmhouse with the generous screened-in porch that served as an extra room most of the year. They mainly raised goats for both entertainment and their business. Tony made goat milk cheese and sold to local restaurants and farmers markets. Amanda produced tried-and-true recipes for a variety of goat's milk beauty products and soaps. Her sales also included farmers markets, a local shop called Sage and Thyme and now, thanks to the assistance of tech friends, she had an online store doing quite well.

"I'm happy to help. The babies are frisky today," Casey noted to Amanda. "Max and Gigi are running around in circles over there. Do you think they know it's officially Baby Goat Yoga at Chestnut Farm time?" said Casey as she redid her unruly hair a little tighter. *I can't wait to see Aunt Laurie at the salon tomorrow.*

"I'm still laughing at Gigi. Your facial expression was priceless when she stayed on your back during the plank pose in the session last weekend," replied Amanda.

"That would've made such a comical photo!" said Casey.

The trendy exercise class was extremely popular for everyone involved. The fresh air and beauty of the farm provided the perfect setting for enjoying outdoor yoga with baby goats.

"I knew the class would be a success," Casey gushed. It's a reprieve from being in my law office wearing heels and a suit all day. Practicing yoga with baby goats is a highlight of my week, and I'm learning so much from Valerie and Karen, the instructors. The goats are so darn cute, jumping all over the place and burping. Hee hee - It's so much fun!"

Just as the previous week, the yoga session brought laughter and joy for every participant. Amanda was armed with her phone and managed to capture photos this time. Gigi was her usual little feisty self and managed to jump on the backs of several surprised yogis, including a new visitor named Susie. Luckily, she was jovial and unfazed by the special attention from the active goats.

The next day, Casey walked into Citrine, the hair salon owned by her Aunt Laurie. "Hey, Casey, it's wonderful to see you again," welcomed the receptionist, a dark-haired beauty with high cheekbones and soulful eyes. Beverly started out sweeping the floors when Casey was a young girl and often visited the salon. Some days Casey would bring books and sit quietly while her Aunt Laurie worked. Other days, Casey danced around, entertaining customers with impromptu performances, her auburn curls bouncing and jiggling as she pantomimed and curtseyed. Casey remembered Beverly as fascinating; her colorful beads, bangles and sparkling sterling earrings that caught the light. Her long, flowing outfits typically had earthy hues and a touch of fringe. She floated around the space, ensuring that everyone was comfortable. Sometimes, Beverly would sit with Casey and just weave a tale or two from her vivid imagination. Beverly loved horses, and the stories often included riding on a beach at sunset or in the forest with sunbeams streaming through the trees. Her stories made Casey feel wrapped in love. Beverly's voice was captivating.

Beverly gradually convinced Laurie that she needed to make a few changes to the salon. They enhanced the reception area to welcome clients with soft chairs and gentle lighting. She also realized that sometimes it was necessary for clients to bring their children. A practical space with crayons, books, and puzzles welcomed little ones in the corner, next to the window. It was a natural fit for Beverly to step into the role of receptionist and general manager. Before long, salt lamps added a warm glow, and crystals lined the windowsills. A sound system was installed and flute music drifted throughout the salon creating a zen atmosphere. The chatter of clients and stylists laughing at whatever stories were being told bubbled through the air on the hum of hairdryers. It was a perfect balance.

"Your aunt is in the back doing inventory but will be out in a minute. You can head into the shampoo area and Gina will get you started," said Beverly.

Instead, Casey popped her head into the storeroom to find her aunt and gave her a lingering hug. "It's been way too long, Aunt Laurie. We need to catch up. Any chance you can take a break later and meet me for lunch?"

"I was going to ask you the same, my dear. Let's see if Bryan has an open table later this afternoon. Bryan's Cafe was the most popular and, therefore, the busiest place in town. Customers loved the casual atmosphere, friendly service, and homemade items on the menu. It just so happened that Casey was his number one server a few years back, and he always seemed to find room for her, even on the afternoons that bustled. "I'll send a quick text to Bryan and see what he says."

As Casey walked towards the shampoo area, she felt especially good vibes. Beverly, who studied various forms of intuitive practices, had introduced herbs, crystals, and natural healing to Laurie. "Being here always makes me feel soothed and calm," Casey said to her aunt. "I also love the rainbows dancing on the walls. They are so joyful," she added.

"Yes, I hung the newest crystal prisms in the

bay windows out front a few months ago. We have rainbows every morning. Sometimes they appear even on cloudy days," responded Aunt Laurie with a wink.

Ding." Bryan's looking forward to seeing us and can seat us at two p.m."

Casey smiled as she noticed that her aunt was pleasantly rounded and soft where she used to be firm. She hadn't taken the time to really look at her lately, but still recognized the tie-dyed Bob Marley t-shirt, which had been a favorite for years. *Her shirt is looking worn and slightly thin in spots. It was bright and new when we went to the beach together. How long ago was our beach trip?*

Her aunt's long, wavy grey-streaked hair was haphazardly pulled back into a low ponytail. Aunt Laurie spent her life making others beautiful via her talented stylist hands. However, she rarely felt the need to do anything to her own hair but trim the ends, and only when the other stylists insisted. Her timeless smile was the only makeup she wore.

Aunt Laurie said, "Here, come sit in my chair and tell me what we are doing today, Casey. Your glorious hair is getting long."

"It feels so good to be sitting here with you," Casey shared with affection. Casey was raised by and had lived with her Aunt Laurie since she was a toddler. They were basically mother and daughter, and the salon Casey's second home. It had provided their livelihood and, thankfully, Laurie learned not only the skills of a great stylist but had the business sense for success.

"I was hoping you could trim a few inches and add some highlights today," Casey replied.

"What? Are you finally taking my suggestions? I do believe I mentioned a new look way back when you passed the bar exam over two years ago and started dressing in classy suits," chuckled Aunt Laurie.

"I'm tired of trying to tame my hair each morning," admitted Casey. "It usually ends up pulled back, especially during this time of year."

"Let me add a few layers, so your curls will frame your face. It also needs deep conditioning. Some subtle highlights will add a golden warmth and sophistication. I'll leave the length so it can be styled or worn in your usual topknot," she elaborated as she absent-mindedly rubbed her lower back.

"Do your magic, Aunt Laurie. I'll just close my eyes and take in the scent of mint and eucalyptus that Beverly put in the diffuser today. It's heavenly."

As she relaxed, a feeling of well-being and of coming home overtook her. Her eyes closed and private emotions stirred. *Aunt Laurie is the most important person in my life, and she sacrificed so much to assure I had a secure, loving home. If it wasn't for her, I would have never fulfilled my dream of becoming an attorney.*

Laurie was in the zone -- she snipped, re-shaped, and used her skills to transform Casey's unruly, tangled curls. As she worked, thoughts of a happy little girl drifted to her mind. *I still remember all the laughter while reading bedtime stories. Her fun childhood made us both happy.* Another thought entered her mind. *Casey was in tears when her beloved pet turtle crawled away and temporarily got lost in a pile of fall leaves. The relief on Casey's face when Stuart, the turtle, was found! She had empathy and showed kindness towards all living creatures. She's a wonderful lawyer and will help those in need.*

Both Casey and Laurie vowed silently, *I will make time for the loved ones who make my life so blessed.*

"Ok, Casey, open your eyes and behold the transformation," announced Beverly, who was standing behind them gazing into the mirror with a huge grin.

"I think you'll like your new look," chimed in Aunt Laurie.

Casey hadn't realized how much time had passed, as she was so comfortable at Citrine. She had been in her own little world daydreaming about baby goats and days at the beach and the deep love between her and Aunt Laurie. As she opened her eyes, a lovely, polished version of herself stared back at her. A smile instantly spread across her face. "Oh, my, it's me, but better. Thanks, Aunt Laurie! I should have listened to you a long time ago."

With a knowing, pleased look, Aunt Laurie gave Casey another long, warm hug.

They agreed to meet back at Bryan's Cafe later in the afternoon. They both knew they needed the mini-reunion to catch up. Since she was working at a law office in the nearby town of Oak Glen, it made sense to move closer to the office. Casey eventually found a small apartment next to a public park. The location was ideal for her long days at the office, but still not too far from Duck Creek, the only home she could remember.

"Beverly, could you suggest a few essential oils for me? I'm sure Leya will have them at Sage and Thyme. That's my next stop since I'm in town for the day. Sage and Thyme was a favorite shop in Duck Creek and the owners, Tommy and Leya, were friends from years gone by.

"Of course," answered Beverly as she pulled out a notepad and pencil. "I think you can start with some basic aromatherapy. For fatigue and increased focus, you can try mixtures of rosemary, sweet orange, and lemon essential oils. Eucalyptus stimulates the brain and improves energy. If you want even more energy, thyme and juniper berry are good choices."

"Whoa, my head is spinning already. You really know lots about aromatherapy, Beverly. Thanks. I think I'll start with just a few and then go from there. My apartment doesn't feel like a home yet, and I was hoping adding some scents would help."

She replied, "Yes, the use of essential oil blends can enhance the overall sense of well-being. They can be highly effective in creating the home environment you're seeking. You'll definitely feel a difference."

"I'd be happy to come over and help with making the atmosphere feel peaceful. It's what I love to do, and you would really be doing me a favor," Beverly insisted.

"That's a generous offer, and one I'd love to take you up on," responded Casey. "I need a place to escape after the stress of work. Right now, the atmosphere is more like an empty warehouse with cardboard boxes piled from floor to ceiling," chuckled Casey, an audible sigh escaping her lips.

Beverly said, "Call me one day next week and we can set up a good time. I'm excited to help."

"Sounds great. This is turning into a really wonderful day," said Casey, taking another glance at herself in the mirror as she walked out the door, her list of essential oils in hand.

"I'm starving!" proclaimed Casey as she joined her Aunt Laurie at a table in Bryan's Cafe later that afternoon. The aroma from the essential oils was pleasant as Casey placed her Sage and Thyme burlap shopping bag on the empty chair.

"Have a seat. I already ordered us iced tea. I'm so glad we got a table in the corner where it might be quieter. Just look at this place. It's not even lunch hour and practically every seat is filled. We're so lucky to have such a great cafe right here in town."

"Well, I already know I want the Caprese salad to start. Plus, I have missed his shrimp salad so much. I have to order it," stated Casey.

"I see nothing has changed concerning your appetite," responded her aunt. "I never could figure out where you put all that food when you were a little girl. You could eat as much as a grown man and still be hungry an hour later."

Casey shrugged and peeked at the menu to check out anything that might be interesting for dessert. "The cheesecake with almonds and caramel sounds delicious," she responded.

Several old friends stopped by to compliment Casey on her updated hair throughout the course of the afternoon, but now empty tea glasses and used stacked plates filled the table. They sat in comfortable contentment.

"You're never going to guess what I'm doing next weekend," Casey declared.

"Ummm, I see by your silly grin that it's something you are pleased-as-punch over, " Aunt Laurie answered. "Let me guess. You're finally going to buy a new, adult bed?"

"No way. You know I love my twin bed with the bookshelf headboard. I'm taking a class to be a certified yoga instructor. Do you remember when I told you about the baby goat yoga at Amanda's farm? Well, Amanda made the suggestion that I become an instructor. She thinks I'm a natural. After giving it a little thought, I decided that adding yoga has relaxed me, and maybe I can help others benefit as well. As a matter of fact, I have a new neighbor that has shown some interest. Plus, it's been a challenge for Amanda to find instructors willing to drive out to the farm for the Saturday morning classes. I think it will be a win-win situation."

"Baby goats and being outside sounds like a marvelous idea to me, especially since you're in an office most days," Aunt Laurie agreed. "Perhaps this tired old body might even give yoga a second try. I remember when we took that class when you were a teen? I wish you would've told me that hot yoga was ten thousand degrees. I melted worse than the wicked witch in *The Wizard of Oz.* It wasn't pretty."

Quirky Birds

"Good morning, sunshine!" said Jacob to Sophie as they awoke at nearly the same moment. Dudley, their big, energetic golden retriever jumped off the bed with a *thud* and stretched. Ginger, the kitty, was still snuggled under the covers next to Sophie, not quite ready to start her day.

Sophie and Jacob lived on the homestead right next to Amanda and Tony's farm. Actually, Jacob owned the property, but in recent times, the couple shared the space. Sophie owned property on the other side, with a log cabin she moved into right after tragedy entered her world a few years ago.

"What a marvelous morning," Sophie answered as she gave him a big hug. They had slept with the window cracked, and she could feel the cool spring air and hear birdsong. *The sweet tunes of the birds remind me of time spent on the porch with Sonya. I miss her so much.*

Sophie had a twin sister, Sonya, who sadly died during the coronavirus pandemic. It was during this dark period that Amanda and Sophie became friends. It turned into a friendship that, at the time, neither realized they needed, but one they hoped would last a lifetime.

The first time they met, Amanda gifted Sophie an exquisite, raw rose quartz gemstone, the universal stone of love and healing. Unbeknownst to Amanda at the time, it was the first anniversary of the passing of Sophie's sister.

"Sonya and I spent hours outside on the porch swing daydreaming about trips and talking about the future. We never took the time to do much gardening when we owned the brownstone in town," Sophie admitted.

"You are making up for that now," Jacob replied, looking around at yard work in progress. "The sun is bright, and it looks like another productive gardening day." Lots of renovations were recently completed to the inside of the rambling farmhouse, and they had just started planning and implementing the outdoor projects.

Jacob spent his days at his architectural firm in Riverside, a town not too far from Duck Creek.

His free time has been filled with sketching, planning, and hiring crews to transform the farmhouse that had been in his family for generations. He was a master at building structures from the ground up as well as renovating old bones of estates and breathing new life into them.

"I absolutely love the restorations. When your visions come to life, it is a sight to behold. I think the archways are my favorite. Before, the rooms looked like dark boxes, and now they flow together with gorgeous light and vibrance. It changes the whole atmosphere," said Sophie as they headed outside with their steaming mugs of coffee to the big, newly painted, wrap-around porch. The mugs were Sophie's, as were many of the other brightly colored pottery dishes now stacked in the kitchen cabinets. Slowly, they had been moving her things over to Jacob's place. She deemed his stuff "items perfect for donating." He didn't disagree.

"I can see how your ideas out here are proving to be strokes of genius, too," he smiled as they sat comfortably on a glider side by side on the porch.

She laughed, "Right now, all I see are heaps of brambles and piles of dirt. I am very excited about the hydrangea bushes that were covered up by the underbrush. Look how they have shades of blue, lavender, and pink."

"I remember Mom saving coffee grounds for the hydrangeas. I have no idea what that was all about," Jacob confessed with a smile for another memory.

"It has something to do with the acidity in the soil and altering the color of the flowers, I think," Sophie answered. Glancing across the yard, she gestured to one area and suggested, "Let's keep the rose garden in the same location because I know your Mom loved it. I want to add more varieties, with new colors, and perhaps a trellis. What do you think?" asked Sophie.

"The outside is your domain, but the roses do remind me of Mom. If the gardens look as great as the firepit area around back, it's going to be spectacular!" added Jacob with an affectionate hug.

Sophie had contracted a local company to design and build a big circular firepit in Jacob's backyard right after he moved in. It had become a wonderful gathering space for Jacob and Sophie's friends.

"It's taking forever to rip out the dead debris from neglected areas. After all, the gardens have been covered in overgrown weeds for nearly a decade," sighed Sophie.

She pointed to the yard on the side of the house and exclaimed, "I'd like to plant a cutting garden over there. It would be a mixture of wildflowers and brightly colored plants and bushes that would change with the seasons. I'm hoping that it will fill in enough to always have plenty to cut for vases indoors. Having flower arrangements around always cheers me up. I also love to deliver bunches of pretty flowers to friends," she added with a pleased smile.

"The birds confirm your idea," Jacob said, pointing out the chorus of lively chirping, his voice chuckling like a new stream after a summer rain.

Their daily routine worked for them. Jacob went to the office early most days, so he could be finished and home in plenty of time to enjoy dinner together and spend time outdoors before sunset. In addition to the challenging garden transformation, Sophie busied herself by bringing more items over from her cabin. She was adding touches to make the house homier, including her colorful pillows on the couch, a few of her favorite carpets, and her cuckoo clock. Once back inside, Sophie said, "Let's put the clock over here on the wall next to the fireplace." The chimes of the clock comforted her, and Jacob discovered he also loved the musical tune.

"Yes, we'll be able to hear them both upstairs and downstairs from the living room," answered Jacob.

Sophie adored the cuckoo clock because of the memories it held of her trip to the Black Forest in Germany. The many adventures she had with her twin sister is what filled her thoughts while gardening. The shops filled with hundreds of clocks covering the walls with melodious chiming could be heard from the streets. True to their nature, Sophie and her sister, Sonya, selected the exact same clock. It had been in Sophie's home ever since.

The next morning, Sophie headed downstairs to the kitchen, hearing the clock chime seven times.

She descended the stairs as she heard Jacob singing.

"Happy birthday to you, happy birthday to you. Happy birth-daaay, dear Sophie, happy birthday to you," Jacob sang as he poured himself another cup of coffee.

"That's quite a cheerful way to wake up!" she announced as she walked into the kitchen wearing her favorite yellow-flowered pajamas, with her coarsely textured hair still wrapped in her nighttime satin-lined scarf, a grin washing her face in the sunshine.

"Ah, you heard me, huh?" Jacob replied with a shy, embarrassed look. "I was just practicing, waiting for you to wake up, my dear." He folded her into his arms and whispered, "Happy birthday, beautiful."

Jacob prepared her mug of Sumatra with almond milk, just the way she liked it. A bunch of hydrangeas filled a white ceramic pitcher on the kitchen table. A bowl of fresh strawberries from their garden glistened in a sunbeam next to a store-bought shortbread cake on the counter.

"I thought we could have strawberry shortcake for breakfast," he stated hopefully.

Sophie hadn't felt like celebrating birthdays much since she lost her sister. It was a celebration they shared, and it just didn't seem right without her. Life was good, but she usually just let June sixth slip by without fanfare.

"It sounds like a sumptuous breakfast, especially if we have whipped cream," she said with a playful gleam in her eye.

"Well, of course. I know how you like real whipped cream and not the canned kind, so I picked it up yesterday. It's in the fridge, whipped and ready," he proclaimed, very proud of himself.

The delicious breakfast treat was piled high with whipped cream and an extra strawberry on top. "Yum! This is so, so, good. Strawberry shortcake may have to be a new tradition for my birthday breakfast," Sophie declared.

After breakfast, he said, "Come on in here for your next surprise, as he led her into the living room."

"I could get used to your surprises," she said, still holding her coffee mug. Dudley jumped excitedly around the room, thumping his tail on the furniture. He knew it was a special day and was eager to join in the celebration.

There stood the most eye-catching hand-crafted, unique set of wooden shelves she had ever seen. They stood about four to five feet tall, with six small, oval shelves, fanned out, like a spiral staircase. Each shelf was a natural, thick slab of wood, in different hues.

He explained, "I know how much you love trees and found some special kinds of wood, so all the shelves would be different. Look, they are fluid, so you can move them and arrange them any way you want."

"Oh, Jacob, I love it!" She wrapped her arms around him and said quietly, "I also love you and how well you know me."

"One more thing," he proclaimed as he went around the corner and grabbed two small packages wrapped with blue and white polka dot paper, topped with bows of curly ribbon.

She eagerly took the packages and they sat down on the cream-colored leather sofa they'd picked out together. Dudley had finally settled down and was laying half under the coffee table, right next to them. Inside the first box perched a small and realistic, but quirky-looking bird figure. It was a bluebird, wearing a silver necklace, adorned with a chunky-looking pink stone.

"It's a rose quartz. Just like the one Amanda gave you," said Jacob, as a single tear slipped down Sophie's cheek.

"It's perfect," was all she could say.

After admiring the bird for a few minutes, she gingerly set it on the table and ripped open the other package, and it was also a bird. This one was a yellow finch standing on one leg, holding a leaf. The bird's beak was open, with the head back as if laughing.

Sophie cradled the bird gently against her heart, lowered her head and closed her eyes, with an immediate thought of her twin sister when they were children. She uttered a soft sigh of contentment.

"Jacob, I adore them! Do you remember the story about the leaf from my childhood?"

Jacob winked with a clear, "Yup. When I saw the bird with a leaf, I thought of Sonya on the ground in fits of little girl giggles."

Sophie hugged Jacob, bounced off the sofa, and skipped up the stairs. Her heart was lighter than she had anticipated ever feeling on her birthday again. Sonya felt so close now, all because Jacob had honored her presence on what would have been an otherwise lonesome day.

He went to his office with his heart filled with love for Sophie. *The morning went even better than I hoped.*

The remainder of the day was spent in the garden and walking the labyrinth, bare feet caressing each stone, remembering good times with Sonya.

I know your loving spirit is watching over me and celebrating these happy moments alongside me, my dear sister.

Casey and Amanda surprised Sophie with a brief impromptu visit. They were laughing as they struggled with a piece of furniture wedged in the back seat of Casey's jeep.

"I saw this bench in Timeless Treasures a few weeks ago. I think it will be perfect next to the new cutting garden, right along the rock path you mentioned," Casey said in between tugging and laughing.

"Thanks, it's amazing," exclaimed Sophie as they lifted the arm of the bench slightly, smoothly slipping it out of the vehicle.

"It's the size of a loveseat, with both wrought iron and wood construction. The wooden seat is worn smooth with two perfectly curved-out spots for you and Jacob."

"I can't wait to see how the garden looks once it's finished and filled with flowers along with this sweet bench," Sophie said as the two young women headed back to their car.

"Happy birthday," they shouted through the car window in unison, and Amanda turned around to blow Sophie a kiss.

They all waved as the jeep backed out.

Sophie's birthday was unfolding in a way she had not expected. The touching breakfast of strawberry shortcake and handcrafted gifts was a welcome surprise. The visit from cherished friends and an opportunity to dig in the dirt to begin creating the gardens all filled her heart with genuine joy.

Around the flickering flames of the firepit later that evening, four friends, Sophie, Jacob, Amanda, and Tony, had a birthday toast.

"Thank you for the best birthday I can remember in a very long time," declared Sophie, as their mugs clambered together with a *clunk.* "Also, thanks for the new copper mugs. I love this Dark and Stormy drink. What's in it again?"

Amanda answered, "It has ginger beer, dark rum, and lime. Tony and I discovered this delicious drink at a restaurant in Sedona. We purchased the hammered mugs when we had our long getaway weekend last fall. I knew you would like the mugs, especially filled with this yummy concoction."

"Sophie, we really should plan a mini-vacation to Sedona with you and Jacob sometime. The earth's energy is unbelievable there; you would appreciate the intense vibes. We could all hike up to Cathedral Rock together. I felt an amazing tingling and it was later that I found out we were hiking near one of the famous vortexes."

Jacob responded with a head nod, "I'm in."

Tony had been mostly quiet throughout the evening, truly relaxed and enjoying the company. He suddenly spoke up and said, "Is somebody gonna fill me in about the significance of a bird standing on one foot holding a leaf?"

"Only if you explain your obsession with playing with fire," said Amanda, with a smirk. She had noticed that both Jacob and Tony fiddled with throwing twigs in the fire and were constantly, although happily, rearranging the logs.

The men shrugged, oblivious, with no answers. Amanda and Sophie exchanged a quick, playful eye roll in kinship as the flames crackled.

Sophie thought about her sister and started giggling, and Amanda, remembering the story well, joined her, both laughing until they bent over holding their sides. Tony sat there, baffled, while Jacob had a knowing look about the bird with the leaf.

Amanda controlled herself first, so she started to explain. "When Sophie and her sister were little girls, they were playing together and running through a field. Sonya suddenly fell over and was on the ground laughing..."

Sophie took over the tale, "When I turned around to see what happened, Sonya's laughter continued uncontrollably. When she got it together enough to talk, she simply said, 'I tripped over a leaf! 'After that day, it was our personal, inside joke. One of us would just say 'I tripped over a leaf, 'and fits of giggles would ensue. It happened for years. I guess you had to be there."

Tony nodded, and smiled trying to understand the giggles, as the conversation carried on.

"Did Jacob tell you about the new store with the quirky birds? It's run by a man named Noah and it's called The Tree House. It's right around the corner from Jacob's office. You are going to love it. It has a display of pens, like that one you have with the polished wood, and the most incredible handcrafted prism kaleidoscopes. There are original paintings of baby chicks, soulful cows, and marvelous woodland animals by talented local artists, Molly Sims and Brenda Kidera," continued Amanda with excitement in her voice.

"Do they have more of those birds? interrupted Sophie.

"Yes, they are created by two sisters, Heidi and Wendy. The owner calls them the zen sisters. Each bird is unique, with fun and quirky personalities. We'll have to go take a look one day soon, because you do have a few more shelves to fill," Amanda added.

It was getting late and the fire was almost out, with the bright glow of orange coals still sending up swirls of smoke.

Amanda mentioned, "Did I tell you that Casey has decided to take the course to become a certified yoga instructor?"

Sophie had seen Casey at the baby goat event and wasn't the least bit surprised. "I've always been quite fond of Casey. Through her law office, she took care of the permit for the benches I installed on county property along Main Street. She's not only knowledgeable but has really amazing people skills. Casey made a few phone calls and breezed through the red tape I couldn't make heads or tails over."

The friends ended the evening by watching the sky together in serene silence. The clouds floated around the moon, and the sparkle of the bright stars lit up the midnight blue expanse.

Once they were back home and Amanda was getting ready for bed, Tony said, "I found one of your stones today. The stone had rainbows on it. It was by Daniel's Hardware Store, on one of Sophie's buddy benches.

"Buddy bench?" Amanda said with a chuckle.

"That's what I call 'em. Sophie wanted friends and neighbors to gather and talk, right? So, to me, that's meeting a buddy," he said matter-of-factly.

Tony continued, "The rock also had a sun painted on it with the word *shine*. I picked it up and put it next to a tree on Main Street. I saw a young woman with a little boy pick it up. He acted like it was a nugget of gold and plopped it in his dump truck. He seemed very excited.

"It's called a kindness rock, dear," said Amanda, pleased. "It's supposed to make people smile."

Ladybugs

Clare and her two daughters, Renee and Ann, were invited to a rock painting party. Just like their mom, the girls were inquisitive.

"I've heard of painting on paper. Painting on rocks seems weird to me," the youngest of the two stated honestly.

"Should we Google it?" inquired Renee, Clare's nine-year-old, who was showing her leadership skills. Ann had lost interest and was building a LEGO car, adding Minnie Mouse as the driver.

Clare was an attorney, and even though she was very laid back as a mom, Renee and Clare knew that being planned and ready was her approach. Her older daughter was obviously following suit.

"Relax, Renee. It will be a fun afternoon on a

pleasant day at the farm, painting. However, if you really want to look it up now, we can."

"I'll go get my iPad," the little girl with big eyes and smooth olive complexion said immediately. She typed *kindness rocks* in the search bar. "Wow, look at all this information, Mom!" she said with enthusiasm. She held the iPad so her mom could see. "The Kindness Rocks Project is a trend where people paint stones and rocks with insp-..."

"Inspirational messages or sayings," Clare filled in.

"Wait, what does that mean?" asked Renee.

"Inspirational messages are words of encouragement and kindness," explained her mom.

"So we paint pictures and write words on the rocks," Renee interpreted. "There's more. Let's keep reading," she persevered. "The painted rocks are left in public places for people to find." The passage ended with, "The intention is to spread kindness."

Clare smiled at Renee, and said, "I'm happy we did some research. Now we know why Amanda likes to paint rocks."

Renee looked thoughtful for a second and added, "I think Mimi would love this idea. She's always saying that showing kindness and encouraging others is the right thing to do." She continued her conversation, "I have a new friend at school named Mason. He usually likes to keep to himself at recess, but this week we played on the playground together and I'm getting to know him. If we have center time, he does the same really hard puzzle over and over again. Since he doesn't talk much, I think he would appreciate these rocks."

Meanwhile, on the farm, Amanda rinsed off the smooth river rocks she had collected down by the creek. *I'll put these in the sun to dry and get my paints and brushes ready.*

Her easel and paints were in the corner of the screened-in porch, with paint-splattered rags, small sponges, and canvases. She had started painting again after a dry spell. Leaning up against the table was an almost completed painting of a baby goat. *I think her name should be Marshmallow. She's so soft and sweet.* Baby goats made her think about Casey, a young woman Amanda had known forever. Casey was a neighbor who lived near her cottage before she relocated to the farm. Casey was developing skills as a professional attorney, yet had a balanced approach to life that included self-care. She was currently attending classes to become a yoga instructor and planned to teach a class with baby goats at Chestnut Hill Farm, if all went as planned. Amanda made the suggestion when she saw her interact with others during a class recently. *She is a natural with the goats, as well as the yoga students.*

Amanda recently read an article about kindness rocks and decided Duck Creek needed them. She painted a few batches and took them with her on errands to the bank, market, or just to visit friends. *I feel as happy spreading a simple kindness as the people finding these rocks.* She was hooked.

Tony had completed his early morning farm chores. Walking up from the chicken coop, he encountered Amanda strolling among the sunflowers. Reaching out to take her hand, they walked together in silence for a few quiet moments.

"I love the way they put their faces towards the sun," she said to Tony.

"It looks like they are telling each other secrets," he added. "Let's go sit under our tree for a bit," he suggested after a few more moments wandering around the garden.

The big sprawling chestnut tree had been their favorite spot for years. They sat under the boughs in the soft green grass, still holding hands. The squirrels were hopping from branch to branch, playful and amusing to watch.

"We change and grow, make new friends, and even travel sometimes, but holding your hand under our tree will always feel like home to me," Amanda whispered, a sigh of contentment escaping her slight smile. She paused slightly and added, "Tony, I'm sorry if I have been grouchy lately. Sometimes I feel overwhelmed for no good reason."

Tony silently answered with three short squeezes of her hand. It was their shared signal for *I love you.*

"The most precious gift we can offer others is our attention. When mindfulness embraces those we love, they will bloom like flowers." ~Thich Nhat Hanh

There was a big picnic table in the yard where Amanda arranged the paint tubes, brushes, and rags. She added a small painter's palette to each spot, so Clare and the girls could mix colors if they wanted. Amanda set a painting spot for her neighbor, Sophie, just in case she walked over. She speculated, *I think little Annie and Renee will feel like artists with these little palettes.*

Amanda had texted Sophie earlier today and invited her over too, but hadn't heard back. At least she thought she texted her. Lately, her mind was playing tricks on her. A few times last week she forgot to send invoices. Another day she sat down and spent the entire afternoon listening to the squirrels and birds playing. Although taking time for herself was normal, she had been shocked at the hours that flew by without her realizing it. She was in an involuntary trance these days.

"I'll bring out some lemonade, too," she told Tony.

"They might like those treats with a peppermint stick in the lemon," Tony said. He added in explanation, "You know, the candy is like a straw. Have fun painting and talking with the little girls. It might remind you of your teaching days".

"I do miss being around children. No time now for the lemons, but it's a great idea if we have them over again."

Amanda heard the car pull into the driveway and she went outside to greet her guests. "Hello, and welcome to the painting party!"

They walked around back, past the big sunflower garden, towards the shade of the Chestnut tree.

"Hi, Miss Amanda," said Renee, skipping with her younger sister in tow. "We read all about kindness rocks and can't wait to get started."

"That's great news because everything is situated and ready to paint," she replied as she gestured to the picnic table, piles of rocks haphazardly laid out in the center.

The girls ran over with big eyes and looks of wonder as they saw the various choices of paint tubes scattered around and brushes from tiny to large. A rainbow of paint pens stood up straight and tall in mugs on both ends of the table.

"Mom, should we paint pictures first and add words later?" asked Renee with seriousness belying her age.

Clare looked to Amanda for answers. Amanda laughed and said "You really are all set to get started! Would you like some lemonade first?"

"No thanks," said Renee. "I'm ready to paint, and I brought along a list of words, too."

Both Clare and Amanda started laughing as Sophie walked towards them.

Sophie had not seen Amanda's text right away. She had lately discovered that digging in the dirt was almost as satisfying and nurturing to her soul as long strolls in the woods. Most of the physically hard work in the yard was finished, and now the fun part was beginning. For a few evenings in a row, she had needed Tina's Salve, a mixture of dandelions and body oils to relieve her sore muscles. *The last time I required this treatment was a few years ago when I tried to build the stone labyrinth,* she recalled, also thinking fondly of her sister, Sonya. Sophie had built the circular structure in memory of her sister. At the time, it helped to walk the stone path while meditating.

"It was certainly easy to find you. I could hear your laugter from the front yard. What's so funny?" asked Sophie as she walked up to the picnic table. The chuckling women glanced over at Renee's long list of descriptive and alphabetized words and Sophie nodded in comprehension.

Annie was on the ground in the comfortable grass petting a fluffy gray kitty, oblivious to the laughter the grown-ups were enjoying. "Willow, I'd like to take you home with me," she said softly.

"It looks like Renee is going to be the next kindness rock ambassador for Duck Creek," announced Sophie.

The painting party began.

"Look, I painted a bunny with my thumbprint," Renee announced. She was experimenting with the brushes but also was getting more creative. "I want to write 'Hoppy Spring 'on this one. Hey, did you know a group of bunnies is called a fluffle?" she said with a giggle.

"A fluffle?" Annie chuckled. Their little girl giggles were contagious, causing the others to join in.

Sophie painted owls with big eyes that looked surprised. "I wonder if any of these look like my owl friend," she contemplated aloud. "Did I tell you the story of how my owl friend helped Jacob change his mind about selling his farm?

Clare laughed and said, "Are you talking

about a real owl?"

"I sure am," she replied, "and I named him Darius. It was right after Amanda and I found out about the Higgins land being sold. I decided to invite Jacob over for dinner, in hopes of pointing out all the reasons why selling to that big corporation was not a good idea. It was an emotionally complicated evening, but the 'hoot 'of an owl eased the tense conversation. We both realized after Darius hooted for a second time, that we had a mutual connection to the forest and night sounds. The owl brought back memories of Jacob's childhood he'd almost forgotten."

"My mom was so pleased to help out with getting him out of that agreement. Those men who planned to buy the land and build that shopping mall were the epitome of obnoxiousness," Clare said in reply.

"Your Mom, the famous Ms. Ginsburg, was Jacob's attorney hero. You were a great help, too, I understand."

"Are you talking about Mimi?" asked Renee, as she held up her latest rock with neon-colored polka dots and the words 'laugh more 'for them all to see. "You can call her Connie."

They all smiled and Sophie proposed a lemonade toast to Connie, in true party fashion.

Amanda felt content just watching the

others, but then announced, "I'm going to use the paint pens and write words first, then add decorations. I feel like the written words will inspire me to figure out how to illustrate."

"Do you want to look at my list of encouraging words?" said Renee hopefully.

"I'd love to," she exclaimed, as Renee handed her a folded piece of notebook paper she retrieved from her pocket.

"Let's see if I was thinking of the same words as you," she said with a sparkle in her eyes. She read some of them aloud, "breathe, calm, hope, joy, laugh, listen, peace, relax, and smile. Yes, some of the same words are on my mind," she declared, smiling at the little girl. Renee was obviously pleased.

Meanwhile, Annie busied herself mixing only the colors red and yellow. She also had blobs of black and white on her painter's palette, with various paintbrushes lined up. A bunch of very round flat rocks picked out and ready for her creations were stacked beside her palette.

Clare had painted several cute bumblebees and was neatly printing the word kind next to each one. "Get it? 'Bee 'kind--it's a play on words."

They all chuckled in response while enjoying the shade of the chestnut tree and tall glasses of Amanda's homemade lemonade. The squirrels dropped a few nuts on the party, generating more laughter among the friends.

Amanda started singing, "gray squirrel, gray squirrel..."

Annie finished, "shake your bushy tail."

The song initiated more smiles and sealed an invisible bond between the friends.

"Can we have another painting party?" asked Renee. "I have so many great ideas for more kindness rocks!"

Amanda responded, "Sure, but remember we still have to hide all of these."

The few hours had passed by quickly. The gathering was a success. Brightly colored painted kindness rocks galore in all sizes and shapes laid out on the disheveled picnic table.

"These are going to bring happiness!" said Renee, with enthusiasm.

Clare felt relaxed and happy thinking, *The girls really love it here, out on the farm in the fresh air. We should spend more time outdoors.*

In front of Annie, a long row of ladybugs paraded in shades of red and orange, round, happy dots adorning their cute faces.

"I don't need words on mine. Everybody

knows that ladybugs bring good luck." She paused and continued while holding up the biggest, brightest ladybug. "That's what my kindergarten teachers, Miss Herman and Mrs. Lavender always say."

Indeed, the painting party was a huge success. They divided up the decorated rocks, each promising to scatter and hide them around Duck Creek and nearby towns.

As Amanda and Sophie walked with them towards their car, Renee said, "Bye-bye butterfly."

Annie added, "Take care, polar bear."

Amanda replied, without hesitation, "Give some hugs, ladybugs."

With that, a group hug ended the party.

Feng Shui

"Helloo," called out Beverly as she attempted to knock, her totes swinging around and falling off her shoulders.

It was warm and sunny with a gentle breeze outside, so Casey opened the door when she first woke up in the morning. She could hear Beverly calling way back in the bedroom, through the screen door. "I'm coming," she responded. "Here, let me give you a hand," she added when she saw her friend loaded down with bags.

"I brought a few things I thought might add to the ambiance of your new place," Beverly said with a confident smile as she glanced around. This should go somewhere close to the entrance, facing east, to help add abundance and positive vibes," she said, lifting out a small bronzed statue of a laughing, bald Buddha with his hands on his round belly.

"He's charming and will put me in a good mood as I leave each morning," Casey remarked.

"Welcome to my humble abode," Casey said laughing. Beverly saw a stack of cardboard boxes in the corner, with one directly in the middle of the living area serving as a table. "I see you are admiring my table," Casey chuckled. "No worries, I already found a real one and plan to pick it up later today. Have you heard of a second-hand shop called Timeless Treasures?"

"Oh, yes, some of my favorite pieces have come from there. You never know what you'll find in that place, especially the rooms in the back. I could spend hours browsing," Beverly responded.

On top of one of the open boxes was a book, *Misty of Chincoteague*. "This was Aunt Laurie's favorite book when she was a little girl. She used to read it to me, and now it's a family heirloom," Casey said as she hugged the book, so honored Aunt Laurie had graciously passed it down to her.

"Having favorite things around can add peace to space. We'll have to see what else you have in those unpacked boxes."

"Let's take a tour first, so you can see my entire place," suggested Casey. "This is obviously the living room. Did you notice I have this great window overlooking the yard out back? This whole house is divided up into three apartments. The tenants share the yard and the porch is open to all of us, too. So far, I've only met one neighbor, Samantha. She's an interesting musician and super artsy."

"I love the natural light," responded Beverly, as she dropped the last bag on the floor and sat in a buttery soft, navy blue chair. "This leather chair is fabulous."

"It's my favorite piece of furniture, other than my desk and bookshelves from Amanda. Aunt Laurie gave me this chair when I moved into my first apartment. She also gave me that table with all the plants when I came here," replied Casey.

The long table fit under the big window perfectly. It was an antique with distressed carved wooden legs that added character. The dark oak table top currently displayed a big pink plastic tray with tiny, colorful succulent plants all lined up like little soldiers. Beverly took a mental note of the mirror on the wall facing the kitchen stove. She'd explain to Casey about the Yang energies later.

"This area has great potential," said Beverly. "However, I hope you aren't attached to that pink dish tub!" she smirked with a swish of her arm as if to make the tub vanish.

"What? You don't like my splash of plastic color?" Casey giggled. "Let's move into the kitchen area," taking a few steps to the right.

"There are also lots of colors here." As if in warning, she added, "The curtains were already here when I moved in."

"Well, I love the island, and I see there's plenty of sunlight in here, too. You don't see wide window sills like this anymore. It will be perfect for pots of herbs I bought for you. I have dill, thyme, and rosemary in my bag. Plants bring life energy to space," exclaimed Beverly. "Inviting nature into your kitchen is always a good idea."

Casey responded, "Thanks! I can use the herbs for cooking too." She continued. "I kind of like the black and white checked floor. It's retro and trendy, but I'm not sure what to do with the curtains," Casey said as they walked further into the room. Both looking down at the floor for a second, the two women accidentally collided.

They bounced back from one another and Casey looked up at Beverly, regaining her balance. "I just noticed your beautiful necklace. What is that stone? It's glowing against your blue shirt."

"It's a moonstone, and I wore it today because it promotes inspiration. Perfect for our task at hand. I bought this pendant years ago at Twins Silver Dream, the jewelry boutique Sophie ran with her twin sister. I actually have quite a bit of jewelry from them. I loved that many of their beautifully crafted pieces came with a story about the artist. They also offered explanations about the gemstones and the metaphysical qualities."

Casey nodded in agreement, recalling the generosity of Sophie when she gifted her the rainbow selection of fluorite jewelry. "I have a few fluorite pieces from Sophie. She mentioned something about healing properties and promoting self-confidence and positive energy. It was from a collection that she and her sister bought from jewelry artists in Italy, on their trip before Sonya got sick."

The two friends paused and contemplated the gift of life and friendships for a few moments.

"I believe giving jewelry to friends was part of a healing journey for Sophie," Casey said quietly. After a moment, she perked up and exclaimed, "Back to the kitchen."

"The curtains are definitely a splash of color," acknowledged Beverly with a funny scowl.

The poofy, ruffled fabric adorned with giant, red poppies alternating with bold black stripes stood out against the wall with a grimace.

"Oh, my, don't they give you a headache just looking at them?"

Casey laughed and replied, "Well, they definitely aren't growing on me. They're history." And to prove her intention, Casey pulled a chair over, jumped up on it, and removed the tension rod in a quick swoop. Dust filtered through the air as the curtains landed in a heap on the floor. "That was easy!"

"Why are all these appliances on the island? Are you re-organizing your cabinets?" inquired Beverly.

"No, I just keep them there, so when I make my morning smoothie or coffee, I can just put the blender or whatever on the counter and plug it in. It saves me time, but the cords hanging all over do annoy me sometimes," Casey admitted.

"Ah, no worries, we'll find a solution for the appliances and the electrical cords." Looking towards the other side of the kitchen, Beverly declared, "The round table by the window is perfect and the pitcher of sunflowers is joyful."

"I love fresh-cut flowers. They cheer me up, and sunflowers are my favorite. I cut those from Amanda's garden a few days ago. They smile at me every morning," Casey said with delight.

"I really appreciate you coming over to help me with my place. Even with my new diffuser and essential oils, it doesn't have great vibes yet."

"I'm happy to help," she replied, giving Casey a big hug. "I still remember you dancing around the salon when you were a little girl. You had such positive energy. We'll find that magic and bring it here. I promise."

"I made us lunch. Since we are in the kitchen, let's eat before we see the rest and you start your magic," Casey declared.

Beverly replied, "Sounds great. Should I set the table?" *I did rush out without eating today.*

"No need, it's all ready." Casey reached for the cutting board spread with olives and vegetables cut into pieces, with a savory dip in a small ceramic bowl off to the side.

"Can you please put this on the table?" Casey grabbed two glasses and a pitcher of sun tea and placed them on the crowded island. With a look of annoyance, she sighed, "It is cluttered in here."

Beverly filled the two glasses and carried them to the table. Casey had also made a chilled butternut soup. She added a dollop of crème fraiche, and topped the bowls with salted, toasted sunflower seeds and a sprinkling of nutmeg.

"Wow, this is delicious!" exclaimed Beverly. "Where did you learn to cook like this?"

Casey said with an appreciative smile, "Remember, I worked at Bryan's Cafe while going to school? I picked up a few tips and recipes during my time there."

After lunch, they toured the rest of Casey's new apartment without much fanfare, until they reached her bedroom.

"For goodness sake," Beverly said with a baaa haaaa. "Casey Maria Layson, Esquire, you are still sleeping in a tiny twin bed? Is that quilt and stuffed bear from your childhood?" she added with another fit of laughter. "Some updates need to happen here very soon. I suppose you don't have many overnight guests these days? Huh?" she said with an inquisitive look over her reading glasses.

"The shelves on the headboard are very handy," said Casey in weak defense. Casey knew Beverly was right. It was rather obvious.

Beverly looked around the rest of the bedroom and stated, "I know you've recently moved, Casey, so I'm assuming you're not fully unpacked." She gazed at half-filled boxes, artwork leaning against the walls, and massive piles of clothing all over the floor. "Please keep in mind that clutter creates stagnant energy. It can make you feel drained because it blocks the flow of energy in your home," Beverly explained.

"Let's get the clothes hung up in your closet and put away in the dresser. You have a wonderful assortment of professional clothing," she noted as they worked easily side by side. "I know it's an investment to dress professionally for court, so let's be sure your work clothes are placed neatly in your closet." As they collaborated, the friends organized and hung Casey's clothes according to the colors of the rainbow. The yoga clothes were also folded and arranged in the dresser drawers along with her other casual clothing.

Amazed how appealing her closet and dresser drawers had become within such a short period of time, Casey sighed and grinned at the sight of the transformation and empty floor. "I can't thank you, enough!" she exclaimed with joy.

"You'll probably sleep soundly tonight, and you might even decide to purchase yourself an adult bed sometime very soon," Beverly mentioned with laughter in her eyes.

Memory Lane

Annie came home from kindergarten and announced in a bold voice, "It's Halloween month and I want to dress up in a ladybug costume!"

Renee replied, "Yes, it's almost October and it's also my double-digit birthday month."

"Double-digit? What does that mean?"

"I'm going to be ten years old and that number has a one and a zero. That's two numbers - double digits. My teacher says it's a milestone and a big deal," Renee said with tenacity, as she plopped her heavy backpack on the kitchen table. Annie wandered off to her bedroom in search of red clothes still thinking about ladybugs.

"This is a special birthday for you, Renee," said her mom. "What kind of party would you like?

We should start planning the big day."

"Can I have my birthday party at the bookstore?" asked Renee. "It's one of my favorite places."

Her mom replied, "We could check into it, but I was talking to Amanda the other day. She said you can invite a few friends to go play with the baby goats and have a picnic birthday party at her farm. We could give books to your friends as party favors."

"That sounds awesome!" Renee squealed with excitement. "Books and the farm. I'll go start making a list of friends to invite."

Meanwhile, Renee's Mimi had been brainstorming and came up with a creative gift for her double-digit birthday.

Connie Ginsburg turned onto the long driveway where she saw the large wooden sign for Memory Lane Stables. The entrance had an abundance of yellow and orange mums happily waving *hello* in the breeze. There were far-reaching green fields, with horses grazing on both sides of the lane. The harmonious colors of autumn on the treetops surrounding the stables resembled a painting. The white fencing looked like it just received a fresh coat of paint. *I like this place; it's cheerful.*

A young lady with a bouncy blonde ponytail

and faded jeans greeted her as she stepped out of her car. "Welcome to Memory Lane Stables."

"Thanks and good morning," said Connie with a genuinely happy smile. "I'm interested in signing up my granddaughter for riding lessons. Can you help me?"

"Of course. Come on into the office and I can tell you about the stables and show you what we have available," she replied. They moved towards a big red barn. "My name is Bonny and I'm the Operations Manager. Have you been here before?"

"No, but I have a few friends who recommended your farm. A young law associate, Casey Layson, and her friend, Beverly Hopi.

"Yes, Beverly comes here to ride and helps us exercise our older horses," said Bonny. "I remember Casey, too, although it's been quite some time since I've seen her."

Inside, a poster tacked to the barn wall presented pictures of employee associates: Lisa, Jacki, Linda, and Gee Gee, all perched on majestic horses.

It looks like all the employees are women, noted Connie with a look of approval. She preferred to support women-owned businesses.

"You may have noticed the stable is owned and operated by women," she stated proudly, as if reading her mind. "The owner is Arianna Jennings and that was her intention when she opened Memory Lane nearly ten years ago."

"I love to support women entrepreneurs," Connie responded.

Bonny asked, "Would you like a tour before we sit down in my office?"

"No, that's not necessary. I like it here already." She noticed a meadow on the other side of the barn with a rainbow of wildflowers cascading down a slight slope, with long stems craning their necks toward the sunlight. *Yes, Renee will love it here.*

"Well then, my office is right over here," Bonny guided. "Have a seat and tell me about your granddaughter."

"Renee will be ten years old soon. She loves the outdoors and is constantly reading books about horses. I like giving gifts that include an adventure or a fun experience, so I thought horseback riding lessons would be perfect for her birthday. Is a ten-year-old too young for lessons?"

"No, not at all. Some children start lessons as young as six, but ten is really ideal. We have several packages available for various skill levels. Has she had any experience with riding?" Bonny inquired.

"Actually, I don't believe she's even been on or near a live horse, ever," said Connie matter-of-factly. I would definitely say she's a beginner."

"What a fabulous gift. It's going to be an exciting adventure for her," replied Bonny. "We have trained instructors who will explain everything in detail, so she will feel at ease and comfortable from the very first lesson. We also have benches set up near the corrals for parents and grandparents, too, of course, to watch the lessons."

Connie drove home admiring the countryside, very pleased with herself. *This gift will be a complete surprise for Clare, her husband Ethan, and especially Renee. I adore a good surprise.*

The party day finally arrived. "I'm so excited!" announced Renee as soon as she came down to breakfast. "It's a sunny day, and it will be perfect for a picnic at the farm."

Annie was nearby and chimed in, "What's a greeter supposed to do again?"

"You just say hello to everyone when they show up and point to where the party is set up; that's all," Renee explained for the tenth time since yesterday.

"I hope you're hungry. I'm making Nutella crepes with strawberries and blueberries for your special birthday breakfast," said her Mom. "Mimi should be here any minute. She's going to spend the whole day with us. Annie and Dad are already gathering decorations for the party."

Renee did a little twirl with her favorite, floor-length princess nightgown still on, and said, "Best day ever!"

Her mom smiled with delight. *I love that she's still a happy little girl, twirling in her nightgown.*

Mimi pulled into the driveway and parked beside the shiny red minivan. She wore a long colorful cardigan with dark jeans, along with her signature pearls. Her wavy gray hair was in a neat bun at the nape of her neck. This was her absolute most casual attire.

After a delicious breakfast and a few games of Scrabble Junior, the girls, along with Clare, Ethan, and Mimi, piled into the minivan.

"It's a good thing we have the Red Rocket, referring to their van. We all fit fine in here together," said Annie. "Off to the farm!"

Ethan's parents, Pop Pop, and Grammy met them as they parked by Amanda and Tony's farmhouse. They had a much farther drive so they didn't get to visit with them nearly as often as Mimi.

"Happy birthday to you, happy birthday to you!" sang Pop Pop in his deep baritone voice. Renee leaped into his arms for a hug, as Grammy joined in for both the song and the embrace.

Annie was the official greeter for the boys and girls attending the party. She took her role very seriously and enthusiastically welcomed each friend as they arrived. "Welcome to the double-digit birthday party. We're so happy you're here!"

The children played racing games, painted pumpkins, and took turns with the hula hoops. They also got to feed the baby goats and frolicked in the pen with them. The ducklings, who were a few months old, loved the attention too.

"Look at Snowball," said Annie. "She's really showing off today. It looks like she's a dancing goat."

"Freddy is trying to nibble everyone's clothes," said Renee with a giggle.

"Max and Gigi have been running around in circles all morning," said Miss Amanda as she handed out grain to the children to feed the goats.

Mason, one of the children attending the party, was a small quiet boy from her class at school. He usually found friendships to be a challenge, yet the two had become close. They played at recess nearly every day, which was a relief to Mason's family. Renee was one of his first school friends.

"Would you like to feed the baby goats or look at the ducklings, Mason?" Renee asked as she walked over to the Chestnut tree where Mason was alone, drawing circles in the dirt with a stick. "I think I'll stay here," he replied.

The two friends sat quietly under the tree placing chestnuts in a pile. The rays of sunshine through the tree branches made moving patterns on the ground as golden yellow leaves floated downward.

Mason didn't often look at Renee directly, but because he felt comfortable around her he had quite a bit to say lately.

In a serious voice, he announced, "Do you know that chestnuts from this kind of American Chestnut tree can be very sweet? You should save them and roast them. They're very healthy and contain antioxidants."

Almost as an afterthought, he added, just as two squirrels were playfully running up the broad tree trunk, "I'm glad to be at your party, Renee."

She neatly rearranged the chestnuts with him in a circle and they stayed there for a few more minutes together listening to the other children laughing.

The guests enjoyed the party food and sang with gusto as Renee's dad carried out a big platter of decorated cake balls. Instead of candles, they were ablaze with sputtering sparklers, resulting in instant wide eyes and applause.

It was certainly a happy celebration and the kids, both human and animal, were pleasantly tired from the games and activities of the afternoon.

As the children left, Renee said words of appreciation to each guest and gave them a parting present. She couldn't decide on gift books so she picked out blank diaries instead. "Here's a journal for you to write all your happy thoughts, worries, and ideas for the future," she said in explanation.

She had chosen special covers, such as rainbows, soccer balls, and hearts to match each friend's personality. Mason got a green cover with owls because he imparted words of wisdom.

Once back home, Mimi was able to tell Renee more about Memory Lane Stables and how she planned to take her there for the lessons.

"I've always wanted to ride a horse and can't wait to start!" she exclaimed, jumping up and down with excitement.

Connie also mentioned to her daughter, "I pre-ordered a dozen copies of Amanda Gorman's new book, *The Hill We Climb: An Inaugural Poem for the Country.* I want both Annie and Renee to have a personal copy of this poem. When they get older, they'll understand the impact and importance of this brilliant poet."

"Who knows, she may be President one day," Clare replied.

"Can you read to me?" asked a sleepy Annie.

"Of course," said her mom.

They shared her favorite stories, *Just Add Glitter* and *The Grouchy Ladybug* with Annie filling in some of the words she had learned in school.

"When can I ride on a horse?" was her final comment, falling asleep before there was time for the response.

Around the Table

The air held an invigorating crispness as Casey walked through the forest with Sophie and Amanda.

The trees' canopy greeted them with brilliant shades of gold, burnt orange, and deep scarlet, with the usual green pines and cypress adding contrast. Sunbeams gleamed brightly through the boughs creating dappled designs dancing on the soft leaf-speckled ground.

"I'm glad I grabbed a knit wrap. It's a bit chilly," said Casey as she wrapped the oversized navy shawl closer around her shoulders.

Sophie nodded her head in agreement as she buttoned up her jean jacket, comfortable in her favorite old leather boots and teal scarf.

"Ha! I was just about to take off my sweater," replied Amanda. "The sun feels so good but I'm getting a little too warm."

Sophie and Casey were a bit surprised but just kept walking through the woods on Sophie's property. Sophie noticed Amanda's flushed complexion, and hoped she wasn't coming down with something.

"It's so peaceful out here. I didn't realize the birds had such a variety of chirping sounds," said Casey.

"Yes," said Amanda. "If you listen carefully, especially when it's quiet, you can distinguish the different birds and their songs. Do you hear that melancholy whistle? It's the golden-crowned sparrow. Their songs are one of my favorites."

"Look!" said Casey pointing up. "The birds are swooping, hopping, and fluttering from branch to branch. I guess I never took the time to really watch them before," she said with awe.

Sophie and Amanda chuckled at their friend's response to being in the woods. It was their favorite place and they could see a new admirer in the making.

"Robins gather into small groups and search for berries on the ground and in trees in the fall. Their music is a string of clear notes that sound similar to syllables. I think they sound cheerful," admitted Sophie.

"I have a new friend who is a musician. Maybe we'll plan a visit out here sometime. Sam will appreciate the melodic forest songs," Casey shared. Her thoughts drifted to the evening before with Stacey and Sam. They all lived in the apartment house, next to the park, but Casey hadn't even visited the park yet. The three friends had recently enjoyed a remarkable yoga session under the new moon.

Casey was startled out of her reflections about the previous evening when Amanda offered, "I have the classic *Peterson Field Guide Bird Book* at home. It's helpful to identify the species of birds. You're welcome to borrow it anytime."

Casey politely nodded, still contemplating the moon yoga.

"Speaking of gatherings, Thanksgiving is just around the corner. What would you like me to bring for dinner, Sophie?" asked Amanda, as she used a large maple leaf to fan herself.

Sophie replied, "I'm excited. This will be the first time Jacob and I host a dinner for friends. I think I'll be fine with the turkey and side dishes. However, I'd love for you to make a few pies."

"Sure. Tony makes a wonderful pecan pie, and I can make an apple and pumpkin pie. I have also been experimenting with bread recipes lately. Would you like me to make dinner rolls, too?" offered Amanda.

"That sounds perfect," said Sophie.

The friends took a rest on a big flat rock and watched the water flow down the creek in little ripples. The colorful leaves drifted downward, as soft as feathers, without a sound.

Quietly, Casey gazed at the creek. She was in her own little world, mesmerized by the rippling water.

After a few minutes, Casey blurted out, "Between spending time with the baby goats at Amanda's, riding the horses at Memory Lane Stables, and being out here with you guys, I may be turning into a tree-hugging, country girl."

Casey smiled, then leaned back, gazed up at the trees, and felt the sun on her face with a *sigh*.

Her friends said in harmony, "Welcome to the club."

Sophie returned home to Jacob with Dudley dashing across the yard. The dog's sheer excitement was evident each time the frisbee flew through the air. Sophie had a true sense of family as she gazed at the two playing.

She chuckled softly to herself as Dudley

cocked his head to the side and suddenly took off after a bunny in the opposite direction of the frisbee. "Does he ever catch them?" she asked Jacob as she walked across the yard towards him.

"Never, and if he did, he would simply make a new friend."

Autumn came in gently, with the cooler weather welcomed by an array of asters, mums, and sunflowers on Jacob's family homestead. After his parents passed away, he had inherited the farmhouse and a large amount of acreage, right on Duck Creek where he grew up.

The porch swing held Sophie's blankets piled for chilly evenings. Her eclectic variety of pots overflowed with plants and colorful asters to greet guests as they climbed the front steps.

Sophie and Jacob arranged golden woven placemats around the expansive table, a dark mahogany antique they recently purchased.

Sophie noticed her kitty, Ginger, lounging in a bright spot of sunlight coming in from the window. Dudley tried to inch his way into the warm beam but was told with no uncertain terms that he was not welcome and to go find his own ray of sunshine.

Blinking and bringing herself back to the task, Sophie stated, "I can't believe how perfect this table looks in here. I think all the different chairs add character, don't you?

"As soon as I saw it in the window at the shop downtown, I knew it was the one. With a little loving care and a bit of staining and polishing, it turned out great. I was disappointed that it didn't have chairs, but you solved that problem."

Sophie replied, "I was lucky to find them at Timeless Treasures."

The table setting included a place for each guest with a personal Quirky Bird made by the artists, Heidi and Wendy. They were talented sisters who created a variety of ingenious bird figurines in all colors and sizes, in clever poses, to fit various personalities and attributes.

"There's no need for names," she told Jacob. "Once they see the birds, they'll know which one is meant for them," she said with a pleased smile.

Sophie had gone shopping at Noah's Treehouse several times during the summer and the beginning of fall. During each trip, her hope and dream of finding special birds for each friend came true.

"You look like a child at Christmas, setting out those little birds," laughed Jacob.

"I think these Quirky Birds are my favorite part of hosting Thanksgiving!"

Casey arrived sporting her stretchy yoga pants and a new soft, tunic-length purple cashmere sweater. Her fluorite pendant looked especially stunning against the royal purple. She carried a colorful flower arrangement up the steps. Noah, Jacob's new friend, walked up the path with two bottles of wine and helped her with the door. They casually introduced themselves to each other, and Noah was immediately smitten. *Do people really fall in love at first sight?*

The house was soon vibrant with easy conversations among the best of new and old friends. The music, wine, and traditional meal added to the festive, but casual, atmosphere. Ginger, Sophie's kitty, hid in the bedroom as Dudley curled up on the floor in between Jacob and Tony. The friendly dog knew exactly where to sit for the best opportunities for scraps to be tossed his way. Both Tony and Jacob sported blue plaid flannel shirts with jeans and looked like they could have been brothers.

The friends laughed, thrilled at the bird gifts and Sophie was absolutely correct. They knew exactly which figurine was meant for each friend. All the guests joyfully commented over Sophie's clever and thoughtful decorating and place-setting idea.

Sophie was pleased that Ruthie-Louise had graciously accepted the Thanksgiving invitation as soon as she received it. They had only chatted via text messages and phone calls recently, but both felt an enormous draw to each other.

"I love the benches you had built and placed around town," was one such phone conversation. "It brings people together," she exclaimed. "I knew my contribution would be in good hands with you, Sophie."

One evening after she heard from Ruthie-Louise, Sophie and Jacob cuddled next to the fireplace. Sophie explained, "She will always be a part of our lives, Jacob. Sonya's heart is beating and alive inside Ruthie-Louise."

After the death of her twin, Sophie discovered that thanks to Sonya's heart donation another person lived. The transplant recipient, Ruthie-Loiuse, tracked her down and they had an emotional visit. To show her gratitude, Ruthie-Louise left a generous sum of money for Sophie to "spend making others happy."

After the donor conversation, Jacob held Sophie for a long embrace. *You will always be a part of my life, my darling. I want to marry you.*

After the meal, the friends gathered around the fire pit late into the evening. The wine still flowed as Casey looked skyward and pointed out the beautiful bright moon. She sat next to Noah, who had been gazing at her with admiration. Quite content being with friends, Casey was totally oblivious to Noah's attention. Amanda noticed and inwardly concocted possible future scenarios. Casey's mind drifted to the lovely evening she spent with her neighbors, Stacey and Samantha, under the moon practicing yoga.

"I have an idea," Casey interrupted the silence. "Maybe we can plan a yoga under the moon for the night owls."

"That sounds like an alluring idea. Right now, my belly is full of wine and delicious food, and I can't think about yoga. Let's look at the calendar another day and make plans for when it gets warmer out," suggested Amanda.

Casey responded with a head tilt and a quick, "sounds good".

As the friends began to gather belongings and call it a night, Amanda and Tony remained, collecting wine bottles, and folding blankets after a satisfying day together.

The various sized jam jars with twinkling champagne colored tea lights led them back to the house, through the moonlit yard. Jacob bent over and blew out the candles as they went, noticing how a few plants glowed silver among the dark shadowed garden.

The following morning, Sophie and Jacob slept in, with even Dudley content to snuggle late as the sun rose lazily.

When they finally ambled downstairs, relishing in the slow start to their day, they admitted happily to having agreed to Amanda and Tony's offer last night to help clean up. Their home was tidy with everything put away from hosting Thanksgiving dinner.

Turning on a classic rock oldies station, the two headed out through the house to the porch with leftover pie and coffee. *Love Will Keep Us Alive* by the Eagles sung out from the stereo.

"Hey! Jacob! Where did all these birds come from?" Sophie exclaimed, shocked to discover a whole collection in the living room as she moved towards the porch. "I'm sure our friends took the gifts with them last night," she added, perplexed.

"You were so busy buying gifts for everyone else, you forgot about filling your birthday shelves for you and not our guests. So, I asked Wendy and Heidi to keep track of all the Quirky Birds you bought. They agreed to make a duplicate of each figurine for you."

Sophie set her pie plate and coffee on the table and picked each one up carefully, with great admiration.

Jacob watched Sophie and a renewed love for her filled his heart. *I want to spend the rest of my life with this incredible woman.*

A small white dove held a tiny red heart for Ruthie-Louise.

For Amanda, a bluebird grasped a miniscule paintbrush with paint dripping on a wing.

A slightly larger bluejay held a fish in honor of Tony.

Casey's bird, a sparrow, comically stood on one leg in a yoga tree pose.

Both Sophie and Jacob were caught up in the moment and emotions took over as they spoke of the blessings they shared.

"We are so lucky and fortunate to be together," whispered Jacob.

Sophie gave him a kiss and said, "Yes, I am thankful for us."

After refreshing their cold coffee, Jacob and Sophie finally made it out to the porch swing, with the rich aroma wafting around them. They cherished the beautiful setting and rocked to and fro gently for a few moments, silently grateful for each other. Overflowing with adoration, Sophie grabbed Jacob's hand and turned towards him. "Let's get married!"

The two soulmates stared into each other's alluring brown eyes for only a few seconds before he answered, "Ok, yes, let's get married."

They started laughing as Dudley ran down the porch steps and back up. He sensed something important was happening.

Jacob kissed her on the cheek. "Don't move; I'll be back in a minute," he said spontaneously, as he sprinted back inside the house.

Although she had been in love with Jacob for quite some time, she had not planned the proposal. *I can't believe I just proposed to Jacob. Oh my*, feeling flabbergasted she laughed at herself. *This is what crazy love must be all about.*

He returned, bent down on one knee like an old-fashioned gentleman and opened a black velvet box.

"Jacob, it's absolutely exquisite."

"It was my mother's diamond and I had it reset a few months ago. I was just waiting for the right moment. It seems, beautiful lady, it was you that found the perfect moment, now, didn't you?" he said teasingly.

She admired the sparkling cushion-cut diamond set in white gold with small, brilliant blue sapphires adorning the sides. It was elegant and not the typical diamond solitaire most popular for engagement rings.

"I wanted something special, just like you,"

Jacob said quietly as he slipped the ring on her finger. Their slow, deep kiss whispered of a future filled with love and intimacy.

He paused, with a slight blush spreading over his cheeks, took both of her hands in his, and stated, "I honestly have been planning a proposal but I guess you beat me to it!" She glanced down at her sparkling finger and still couldn't believe her spontaneous proposal.

Karma

Casey was tickled. She successfully completed the advanced course and officially qualified as a Certified Yoga Practitioner.

Still winter and cold, Baby Goats at Chestnut Hill wasn't happening anytime soon. However, a couple of months earlier she met new neighbors and they still had an occasional yoga practice in her living room. She enjoyed using the disciplines she learned in her studies with her new yogi friends, Sam and Stacey. The open conversations and tea afterward were becoming special times.

Casey couldn't wait to share the certification news with her Aunt Laurie and Amanda, too, of course. Aunt Laurie was always the person she told updates to first.

Laurie knocked on Casey's front door holding

a salt lamp. It was the type with a small bowl that held translucent rose-gold chunks of salt. When plugged in, the glow was lovely. This particular lamp, an abundance bowl, produced negative ions to purify the air. The abundance was also known to amplify love, finances, and other areas of life.

"Hi! Come on in. You know you don't have to keep bringing me gifts when I invite you over," said Casey.

"I know, but I saw this and thought of you and your newly zenned-out apartment. Beverly was so pleased to help bring a peaceful vibe to your home."

"You are so sweet, Aunt Laurie. Actually, this visit is a celebration," Casey declared.

They settled on the couch next to the display of healthy colorful succulents, now arranged in a beautiful copper tray with handles molded into the shape of stars and moons.

Aunt Laurie wore old overalls that looked as though she'd had them for decades. Her silver-flecked hair was brushed and spread in long lustrous waves across her shoulders and down her back.

"Your hair looks beautiful," Casey said as she handed her a cup of tea.

"Thanks. One of the girls at the salon insisted

I needed a trim and deep conditioning, so I had a pampering session."

"What are we celebrating?" Laurie asked her niece.

"Do you want to hear about my recent accomplishment or the adventure planned for the future?" Casey asked with a little gleam in her eye like she had a secret bursting to get out.

"You aren't moving out of the area, are you?" her aunt said, trying to hide a sudden sadness.

"No! No, the news has nothing to do with relocating," Casey gushed. "Goodness, I didn't mean to startle you, Aunt Laurie."

Laurie breathed a sigh of relief, took a sip of her tea, and said, "Then your accomplishment news first, please."

Casey proudly said, "Ta-da! I finished my class requirements and I'm now a certified yoga instructor," demonstrating a mighty warrior pose with a flourish.

"That's wonderful news! Does Amanda know yet?"

"I wanted to share the news with you first. Plus, yoga at the farm isn't scheduled until spring when it's warm enough to be outside with the class."

"Speaking of Amanda, I made her famous cinnamon buns. Would you like some?" asked Casey.

Laughing, Laurie admitted, "I can smell them but I thought you had a cinnamon candle burning in the kitchen! Could you hear my stomach growling? Yes, I would love a cinnamon roll, and Amanda's recipe is the best."

Casey brought out the buns, still warm from the oven.

"I'm in heaven," declared Aunt Laurie. "You're a girl of many talents, my dear Casey." Taking another bite, she added, "These are absolutely decadent."

Icing dripped down Casey's chin and a little on both her yoga pants and palm tree sweatshirt. Stuffing a large piece of the delectable treat in her mouth, she replied, "Thanks," grabbing a napkin, half mumbling her words.

"Now for the adventure," Casey said in a low controlled voice, mimicking a radio announcer. Picking up her phone, with a few clicks, reggae music played on the speakers.

"Are we having a dance party?"

"Maybe," said Casey as she handed her Aunt Laurie a bulging manilla envelope and simply directed, "Take a look inside."

As Laurie accepted the mysterious package, a seashell fell onto her lap.

"Look at what else is in there," Casey encouraged her aunt.

Inside was a small bottle of suntan lotion, a new tie-dyed Bob Marley t-shirt, more seashells, and a brochure to a resort in Jamaica.

"Whaaat?" Laurie stammered.

Casey announced with enthusiasm, "We're going on a tropical vacation. Pack your bags because we leave next week!" She jumped up and gave her aunt a great big hug while swaying with her back and forth to the beat of the music.

"Beverly already knows and your schedule is cleared," Casey added before Laurie could object.

At that moment a new song came on and they moved and sashayed to the upbeat tune about being worry-free.

"I guess we are having a dance party!" Laurie declared.

Casey happily embraced her aunt as the song came to an end.

The day before the trip, Laurie insisted Casey visit Citrine after work so she could style her hair for the vacation.

"My bags are packed and ready," Casey told Laurie as she worked her magic with the neat, intricate braid.

"I just have to add a few paperbacks to my carry-on," replied Laurie. The two travelers were set and excited about the beach vacation. This was the final preparation with matching French braids, with Casey's amber curls tamed and Laurie's natural hair smoothed.

Before they knew it, Casey and Laurie were at the airport with time to spare. Laurie hadn't traveled in a long while and was a nervous Nellie, insisting on leaving extra early.

"Is it really toasty in here, or am I having a hot flash?" Aunt Laurie asked as they waited to check their luggage at the airport. She fanned herself to no avail.

"No, it's very hot, like the air conditioner isn't working at all," responded Casey, balancing her carry-on with her purse and suitcase as the line slowly inched closer to the check-in desk.

The lights flickered several times and an announcement came on, "Attention: The terminal is experiencing temporary technical difficulties. The wait time will be longer than usual as the attendants must enter your information by hand. Thank you for your patience."

"Can somebody please fix the air-conditioning?" a voice yelled from the back of the line.

A general sense of moaning and groaning permeated the area. Employees reassured the travelers that the problem was being addressed as quickly as possible.

"It's going to be so great at the beach," said Casey. "This warm air is just preparing us for sunshine and calm waves. Close your eyes and think about blue water, soft sand, and palm trees swaying in the breeze."

"Aah, thanks so much for this vacation. So what if we have to wait in line a little longer. It will be worth it," agreed Laurie.

An older man with a helmet of sandy beige hair shoved his way towards the front of the line. Sweating, with a rumpled suit and coffee stains on his dangling tie, he dragged a large suitcase, rudely bumping into others. A scrawny, younger man with skinny elbows juggling golf clubs followed closely behind him, like a caddy. The assistant could be seen across the room with his spiked red hair protruding in every direction.

Aunt Laurie leaned in close and whispered, "He looks like a barbequed chicken wing."

Casey and Laurie chuckled at the private joke.

"Excuse me, I NEED to check in NOW," hollered the older man.

"Sir, please step back and return to the end of the line. You have to wait your turn like everyone else," instructed a sweltering airport guard.

"I can't wait! Check me in now!" he demanded, turning towards the agitated crowd in line behind him and grumbling something about previously owning a private jet.

Embarrassed, his assistant slumped over in defeat, letting the golf clubs fall to the floor with a metallic *clang.*

"You idiot! Take my suitcase and find somebody in charge. Get me checked in NOW!" he shouted, stomping away empty-handed.

Finally, the annoying murmuring ceased for a moment and everyone looked at the reprehensible traveler in disbelief. Frightened children clung anxiously to their parents 'legs. The growing, diverse group became disgruntled and began complaining loudly until the atmosphere grew hostile.

Laurie smiled at Casey and winked, as the fellow travelers fidgeted, but failed to move ahead. The two women knew each other so well. They had an entire conversation with only their eyes. In essence, they were both contemplating a saying Laurie shared with Casey as a teen:

**"You must not lose faith in humanity. Humanity is like an ocean; if a few drops of the ocean are dirty, the ocean does not become dirty."
~Mahatma Gandhi**

"Whew! I'm so happy to be sitting down," exclaimed Laurie, next to Casey in the cool, roomy row in the front of the plane.

"A little kindness goes a very long way!" Casey replied as she sipped a flute of chilled, sparkling champagne.

They were polite, pleasant and thanked the strained, exhausted airport employee for her hard work when it was finally their turn in line.

"We appreciate you, Ella," Casey said, as she read the employee's name tag. The tall woman with the neat, short bob and professional clothes paused and smiled as she painstakingly checked them in.

Low and behold, they were upgraded to first class for the non-stop flight to Montego Bay.

Meanwhile, the helmet-head, whom they suspected sported a toupee that had now awkwardly shifted to one side, still moaned and groaned. Sitting begrudgingly in the row behind the restrooms in an aisle seat, the other passengers ignored his whining. His knobby legs extended to the side, while flight attendants repeatedly told him to put them in front of him, out of the way. Next to him, squished in the middle seat, sat a young mom with an adorable, but cranky, baby. The obnoxious man's traveling assistant enthusiastically chewed a wad of neon-green chewing gum, undisturbed by the crying infant or the continuous slamming of the restroom door.

Casey held up her second flute of complimentary champagne and grinned, "Cheers to our luxury first class seats!"

"Here's to us!" said Laurie and added with an unintentional snort, "I'm still chuckling about the guy at the airport who resembled a chicken wing."

Their vacation commenced on a positive note, with laughter and bubbly.

Turquoise Cottage

Casey and Laurie arrived at the all-inclusive Beach Jewel Resort shortly before lunch and were escorted to their bungalow by two young, energetic, friendly, dark skinned men with thick black hair. A look passed between the women, and an ever-so-slight raise of the eyebrows from Aunt Laurie caused a burst of laughter. Casey beamed at her aunt as the muscular hunks carried their luggage through the door with ease. They wore uniforms of board shorts, flip flops, and soft cotton t-shirts that clung to their biceps and toned backs.

"Let's just leave our luggage for now and go explore," said Casey, with excitement.

"I can't believe we are staying in this adorable turquoise cottage!" exclaimed Laurie.

As they wandered around the back of their

home away from home, Laurie pointed and announced, "Look, we have hammocks." She then suggested, "Relaxation should be the theme of the week." she suggested.

Casey was so very pleased with her choice of vacation spots. It was everything she dreamed it would be.

I wonder where this path leads? They were surrounded by beautiful trees of every shade of green and large, fuschia colored hibiscus flowers. The native lizards crawled on tree trunks and vivid, colorful birds nestled in the branches.

"This is pure perfection!" Casey murmured to her aunt, who was right beside her looking at the amazing expanse of beach. Small tiki huts and comfy padded lounge chairs spaced out on the nearly empty area, palm trees swaying in the gentle breeze nearby.

Laurie exhaled, not realizing she had been holding her breath from all the excitement. She grabbed Casey's hand and declared, "I love it here."

Casey responded, "You totally deserve this vacation."

"I don't think I've ever seen a more beautiful beach. The calm waves are true azure, with the sun sparkling and dancing," Laurie exclaimed.

Holding hands, they walked along the beach

for a while, watching the tiny fish swim around their feet. The sand was white and soft and the sun warm and inviting. The soft waves ebbed and flowed easily and predictably as the two began to match their breath with the rolling of the tide. Feeling the serenity, the laughter of a few children playing in the surf was the only other sound.

"Our traveling clothes are getting wet and soggy," noticed Laurie. "Let's go change, unpack, and then find the restaurant for lunch," she added.

Casey slipped into a soft gauze sundress with ties at the shoulder. Laurie wore a new tie-dyed t-shirt with linen capris. Casual, flat sandals made for easy walking. Venturing down more paths, they discovered sherbet-hued cottages tucked away along the palms. A tiny, lemon-yellow one stood out next to an orange creamsicle house with a front porch. A young couple sat on a porch swing, sharing a coconut drink with two straws.

Throughout the resort, they came across several pools with fountains and noted a few hot tubs hidden among the beautiful landscaping.

"Let's come back here later and enjoy the hot tub," said Casey.

In the shade stood a small white and robin egg blue ice-cream cart, powered by an old-fashioned pink bicycle. On the side in a curvy font was written, *Cream Cruiser*.

"Look at these incredible ice-cream sandwiches. They are made with colossal cookies and have rainbow sprinkles," exclaimed Laurie.

"I think you'll find they taste even better than they look," said a pretty young woman seated next to the bicycle. "Hi, I'm Katherine. Please let me know if you have questions. All the choices for today are right up here," gesturing to the handwritten menu.

"Thanks very much, Katherine. I don't believe we can resist," said Casey. "Which kind would you like, Aunt Laurie?"

"Let's get one double chocolate with peanut butter and an oatmeal raisin with a coconut sammie, to share," replied her aunt.

"Ha! Peanut butter for protein and oatmeal for fiber, right?" added Casey with a thumbs up.

Their part of the resort was secluded, but this section bustled with young families and groups of all ages. They leisurely ventured through the area, strolling, after indulging in the massive ice-cream treats.

"Look over there at that open-air restaurant, right on the beach," Casey said, pointing to tables with striped umbrellas.

Laurie responded, "We can relax and watch

the waves as we eat lunch. I really do love this resort. We should do dessert first for every meal."

Casey responded, "I like your vacation style, Aunt Laurie."

After the scrumptious ice-cream sandwiches, their lunch was limited to splitting an excellent seafood ceviche paired with a local white wine.

With all the exploring and traveling, they turned in early that evening, exhausted, but happy. Open windows invited in the sound of the sea and lulled them to sleep.

The two women awoke early to the sound of the surf-like music in the air, a constant rhythmic crescendo and decrescendo of the island pulsating to the strengthening rays of the sun.

"Let's take our coffee and sit on the beach," suggested Casey.

They had agreed to keep the trip casual and packed light, bringing only simple dresses, comfy clothes, and definitely no make-up.

"I'm not ready to get dressed," admitted Aunt Laurie. "Don't our nightgowns look just like beach cover-ups?" she suggested with a giggle.

With turquoise patterned ceramic coffee cups in hand, they walked down to the beach still wearing the oversized t-shirts they wore to bed.

"We have the whole beach to ourselves," smiled Casey.

With butts in the sand and legs stretched out, they sat in total contentment.

"This is my favorite time of day at the beach," Laurie declared with pleasure.

Casey replied, "Our part of the beach is so peaceful, especially in the morning."

Further down the surf, it was more crowded. Volleyball games, rambunctious teens, and large families started gathering in the morning sun.

Laurie nodded and smiled in reply.

They started each day with gratitude, on the beach, the sun shining on their faces. "I treasure these mornings with you," said Casey.

Some days they prepared coffee and a light breakfast in the cottage, other days they enjoyed mimosas and being served at the beach-front restaurant.

"Hello, Ajani and Bede!" Laurie and Casey greeted their new friends early one glorious morning.

"Gud mawnin," replied the brothers. "It's another perfect day in paradise," said Bede, in his alluring Jamaican accent.

The brothers dutifully raked the sand of the resort bright and early each morning. Through conversations one day, it was discovered that they had cousins that also worked on the resort. In Jamaica, it was a cream-of-the-crop job, and they were fortunate to have worked there since its opening, twelve years ago.

"Do you ever get a vacation or time off to travel?" inquired Laurie.

The brothers laughed and Ajani answered, "Why would we ever want to leave? It's heaven here. Although we do have picnics on the beach with our families when we have a day off."

As they swiped through photos on their phones, the new friends proudly introduced Casey and Laurie to their extended families. The guys enjoyed showing off their lovely wives and telling a little about their home life. Their adorable, smiling children were building sandcastles with buckets and seashells in the photos.

After gently bobbing in the calm sea and long walks on the beach, Casey and Laurie occasionally stopped at the Lazy Lizard for freshly-made smoothies. The workers were friendly and enjoyed joking and talking with them.

The first time was an experience. The smoothie shack was situated close to the beach among a cluster of palm trees in the shade. A hand-painted sign showed days and hours of operation, with a nearby chalkboard displaying the specialty drink of the day.

When they arrived at about 10:30 a.m., after a long walk, it wasn't open yet.

"I'm parched and hot!" moaned Casey.

Laurie snagged Casey's hand, laughing, and pulled her back down the path. She led her across the sand to the welcoming coolness of the peaceful sea.

"Here ya go," Laurie said as she splashed the wonderfully refreshing water on Casey playfully.

"Aaahhh," that's much better.

It was an especially hot day, but the two were still dripping and cool as they headed back to the shaded umbra of trees. The sign said they opened at 10:00, but it was still closed and shuttered. A few others milled around, also waiting.

A woman slowly strolled towards the shack, wearing a loose, cotton outfit, which flowed with bright colors. With a dramatic wave of her hand, she let the guests know cool drinks were coming soon.

Another island woman with long braids dragged a cart filled with pineapples and coconuts through the sand. She hummed a catchy tune, in no rush whatsoever.

Eventually, Laurie and Casey learned and accepted that sometimes it was open and sometimes it wasn't. *There was no rhyme or reason when it came to Island Time.*

"The coconut, ginger, and mango blend is so yummy," said Casey.

Laurie declared as she sipped her frozen concoction, "This pineapple with guava and greens is energizing. I may walk a few more miles today." She added, "Then I'll just float and listen to the waves and watch the birds."

The next day they woke to rain.

"I love the way the gentle rain sounds with the windows open," said Casey.

Laurie replied, "I adore how you notice and cherish the small wonders all around us."

They leisurely lounged in their pajamas, drinking coffee and eating sliced mango. Laurie excitedly jumped up all of the sudden, reached into a drawer for a small jar, and set it on the dresser.

"Beverly gave this to me. It's an Aztec Indian Healing Mask. Let's put it on and sit on the porch and hope somebody walks by," she said with a mischievous snicker.

"My face is turning hard and greenish. What's this supposed to do again?" Casey mumbled, as her face was too stiff to talk.

"I think Beverly said something about deep pore cleansing and drawing out impurities," answered Laurie, hardly opening her mouth, then adding, "I think my cheek is cracking."

Finishing off the mango after washing their faces, they felt refreshed.

"Let's take a walk in the rain and rinse off the last of this clay," suggested Casey.

Drenched with glistening faces, they jovially skipped along the surf, holding hands, still wearing their pajamas. Corkscrew curls were escaping Casey's braid, and the breeze was tossing the curls along the sides of her face. She was capturing these moments of joy, saving them in her heart, to treasure later.

Healing Waves

By late-morning the sun was shining.

Relishing time on the beach, the two women enjoyed the sweet and fresh air after the rain. Independently immersed in their books, the hours slipped by. The only movement was the soft breeze and a few couples passing by, cuddling and canoodling.

Walking slowly along the surf, Casey said, "Aunt Laurie, tell me about the time you lived in New York City."

"Oh, honey, that was a lifetime ago."

They strolled slowly along the water's edge, with the warm waves rhythmically washing over their ankles.

"Why did you leave the city?" she questioned.

"Let's have an early happy hour, and I'll finally tell you everything you want to know."

Casey was raised solely by her aunt, with no memories of the days before they lived in the small house next to Amanda in Duck Creek. Every time she brought it up, especially as a teen, Laurie's expression became solemn and she changed the subject. Casey only knew bits and pieces of her past but suspected it was a painful time.

"Happy hour sounds great. I'd also love to know more about my mom's paintings and her life as an artist," Casey added.

As a child, an old guitar leaned up against the wall in their living room that Casey was allowed to strum anytime she wanted, but always had to return when finished. Aunt Laurie mentioned it was from New York and added no details. There were also a few paintings displayed, with more at the salon.

Sitting comfortably on lounge chairs on the beach, angled towards each other, Laurie knew it was time to be honest with her beloved Casey. A glass pitcher of sangria with chunks of local fruit glistened in the sunshine on the nearby table. Drinking from the same turquoise mugs they used for their morning coffee, they prepared for the long-awaited conversation.

"I love that the bar makes fresh, buttery popcorn and delivers it to us with the sangria," said Casey with a reassuring smile. *This talk is going to be difficult for Aunt Laurie, but it's long overdue.*

Laurie put on a brave face and relaxed her shoulders, taking another emotional swig.

Once settled, Laurie smiled and began talking. "I went to New York and moved in with my sister, Jennifer, your mom, right after high school. She was six years older than me, established at that time with an apartment in Greenwich Village."

"That sounds so cool, living in Greenwich Village with the artists and dreamers."

"Your mom had talent as an artist but discovered early on she couldn't make a living painting. She loved the artist's life and stayed in a loft with a group of others for a few years. Yes, some were dreamers."

"Was my mom a hippie?" asked Casey, sipping sangria.

"She was a smart hippie. She was really good with people, as well as being artistic. She landed a job at a bohemian art gallery and worked her way up through the ranks," explained Laurie.

Casey asked, "Did she give up painting?"

Laurie explained, "No, the gallery had regular exhibitions of her artwork. When she was introduced to the owners, her talent was appreciated and they liked displaying and offering her work to the community. Between selling her paintings, odd jobs, and saving, she bought her apartment. She was managing the gallery by the time I moved in with her."

"It's a shame I didn't inherit artistic talent," Casey quipped.

Laurie laughed and continued, "While living with Jennifer, I attended school and learned how to style hair. Once graduated, I was able to contribute to the expenses. Sharing the apartment was a special time in our lives."

Casey asked, "Did you get to know her friends and go to wild parties?"

"Ha! It was a fun time and yes, we partied with artists, free spirits, and musicians but I'm not sure if we were wild."

Casey's mind drifted to Sam for nanoseconds. Her new neighbor was a musician and would adore Greenwich Village.

Laurie got dreamy-eyed and stopped talking for a brief moment.

Casey stood, stretched, and declared, "It's time for a break."

It was breezier than the day before, probably the after-effects of the rain. Perfectly styled French braids were keeping their hair from flying all over, as popcorn blew and tumbled along the sand and the gulls swooped down and claimed the treat. Rolling her shoulders, Casey rose to a tree pose, challenging her balance. Laurie stood and bent over attempting to touch her toes a few times but made it only to her shins. Giving up the exercises, she tossed popcorn with purpose towards Casey, instead. Laurie was laughing as birds took the opportunity to gather and conquer, wrecking the harmonious stance Casey had mastered. Determined, she switched over to a child's pose when she toppled into the sand, joining the gulls.

Once they returned to the lounge chairs, Casey remarked, "Uum, this delicious wine is helping me unwind. I'm ready to hear more if you're willing."

"Before I continue this story, you have to realize the best part of New York was always you," Laurie emphasized her statement with a loving gesture, holding her arms wide open towards Casey.

Reaching over and grabbing her hand, Laurie gave Casey a heartfelt squeeze, also taking a deep breath and a generous gulp of sangria before continuing the story.

"I was walking in Central Park one afternoon after work and stopped to listen to a band performing. The guitar player looked up and our eyes met."

"Your guitar?" Casey interrupted.

Laurie's eyes misted over and she shook her head in confirmation.

"His name was Tom. He had long shaggy blonde hair which was always hanging over at least one of his hazel eyes. We became inseparable in no time at all. It was true love."

Casey blushed with wide eyes. *Why hadn't she imagined her aunt in love?*

"Have you heard of Strawberry Fields?" asked Laurie

Casey answered,"Yes, it's a garden in Central Park for the Beatles, right?"

"Aah, yes, in memory of a former band member, John Lennon. It's also a place where musicians gather to play music and promote peace, just like Lennon," Aunt Laurie elaborated.

Casey prompted, "Did something happen there?"

Her aunt leaned back in the chair, put her head back for a moment and continued, "Tom proposed to me while his friends serenaded with a Beatles love song called, *In my Life*. It was a magical moment in my life and I was so glad Jen was there with a few other friends."

They sat there quietly while her aunt composed herself. Laurie beamed briefly from the memory. The scene in her mind was softly blurred, like the edges of a watercolor painting.

Laurie admitted, "This part of my life has been buried for such a long time." With misty eyes, she looked out over the beach into the never-ceasing waves. "Being near the sea opens and calms my soul. I should have shared my story with you years ago, Casey, but I wasn't ready until now."

Casey nodded as more of the tale unfolded.

"We were so in love. Tom wrote songs and sang to me as though I were the most precious person in the world. Holding hands, we talked late into the nights about our future."

"Aahh," murmured Casey, with a dreamy glance towards the shifting clouds.

Laurie noticed and said, "What's that look?"

"Do you remember my senior prom? Colin, my sweetheart at the time, was a musician. He wrote a song to ask me to be his date," reminisced Casey.

Laurie replied, "Yes, he was also a lacrosse player, right?

"Yep, an athlete and musician. I wonder where he is now?" Casey said curiously.

Laurie smiled and said wistfully, "Back to Tom. It was your mom's idea that he move in with us, so he could save his rent money for our future. It was fun getting to know his friends and band members, who became frequent visitors.

The beach was nearly empty, but when a few families walked by, Casey and Laurie remained in their own world, contemplating the past.

"Within a short seven days, Tom proposed and at the same time your mom found out she was pregnant. We honestly couldn't have been more thrilled with our lives," Aunt Laurie shared. "To our delight, Tom was a big help, especially when Jen and I worked long hours. His music gigs were usually on weekends and evenings, so he was willing to spend the days performing the many chores it takes to run a household. He shopped, cleaned, and was even a decent cook. Pasta with shrimp and pesto was one of his specialties. Your mom ate her weight in Tom's pasta. She was always famished and appreciative of his culinary efforts."

"On the evenings Tom didn't have a gig, and we didn't have company, the three of us had such fun. He played and sang our favorite Beatles 'songs after dinner, with us joining in, and sometimes making up lyrics as we went. Your mom tended to fall asleep on the couch after a few songs, and Tom and I would clean up the dishes and let her rest."

"He sounds wonderful. Musically inclined with culinary skills, a perfect combo," Casey included, feeling honored to be hearing this part of Laurie's life.

Aunt Laurie's smile faded as she continued, "Slowly I began to notice my tip money was disappearing. As a hairstylist, a big portion of my earnings was from generous gratuities, which were usually in cash. I kept that money in a wooden box on our dresser. It was alarming to believe any of our visitors would do such a thing."

Casey squeezed her aunt's shoulder and joined her on the lounge chair, so they were sitting side by side, their toes in the sand.

"One day, I walked into our room and Tom was sitting on the bed with the opened tip box beside him. I felt my anger and disappointment well up, and I was about to question him. Before I had the chance, he jumped up, startled, of course." Turning slightly on the chair, Laurie said, "Casey, his answer was, I found a ten-dollar bill on the sidewalk and was adding it to your tip money."

Shaking her head with a frown, Casey allowed her aunt to continue.

"I stood inside the doorway, looking at him in disbelief. I was speechless. My first thought, is it really him?"

"He hurried out of the room, without looking directly at me, his only words were *Gotta run, I'm late for a rehearsal.*"

Casey topped off their mugs with more fortifying wine.

"I sat on the bed, numb with a realization that the man I loved, adored, and planned to spend the rest of my life with was stealing my cash," Laurie admitted.

"Wasn't that money being used for food for the three of you?" Casey clarified?

Laurie agreed, stating, "That's exactly why it was not only heartbreaking but terribly confusing."

Lifting their faces to the sun, the two women soaked in the strength of the warm rays.

Laurie expelled a deep sigh and pressed on, "The week before you were born, my life completely crashed."

She was determined to finish the story and decided to leave nothing out. Laurie cried softly, as Casey reached over and gently held her hand.

"Tom overdosed late one night after playing with the band at a club in Chelsea. One of the band members gave me his guitar after the funeral."

They held each other and rocked gently in an embrace for a couple of minutes, matching the rhythm of the mellow waves.

"Casey, I didn't even know he had a drug problem. We smoked weed a few times at parties, but that's it. He used my money for drugs and I was completely blindsided, totally clueless. I honestly had no idea," admitted Laurie.

She breathed a heavy sigh and gazed out to the sea. As she released the air, she exhaled the story into the depth of the water, gone forever.

"Aunt Laurie, addicts know how to hide secrets and they also lie easily and can be convincing. Don't feel bad. Addicts are manipulative," Casey counseled with a surprisingly mature tone to soothe her aunt.

The two, as close as a mother and daughter could possibly be, stood and walked along the water's edge. The warm water caressed their feet in gentle waves, cleansing hurtful memories away with the tide.

Laurie went on, "Then, your mom went for a checkup right before her due date. Her breathing was labored, and she was tired all the time. Her doctor ordered tests just as a precaution. They found a mass on her left lung."

"I knew she died from cancer, but I didn't

realize it was discovered before I was born. Wow," Casey replied.

"She tried so hard to be strong. Your mom loved you fiercely from the second she held you in her arms. I promised Jen I'd care for you, and, honestly, it scared the blazes out of me," Laurie confessed as the water washed over her feet.

Casey was quiet, calculating, then noted, "You were younger than I am now and with so much responsibility! I would have been frightened, too."

"During the time your mom had treatments, she wasn't able to work much, but the gallery was generous and kept her on the insurance. I tried to squeeze in more hours at the salon even though I really wanted to be home with you and your mom. We were desperate for the money."

They turned and slowly walked back towards the lounge chairs. Aunt Laurie hesitated and smiled as she recalled a pleasant memory.

She continued, "We had a wonderful neighbor, Marie Locke, who helped take care of you. She was a retired educator and you became great buddies. You called her Ree Ree. When you turned three, she organized a finger painting birthday party. You can only imagine the mess. She spread a shower curtain on the floor and suggested you and the other toddler guests wear your bathing suits."

"Baaa haaa. I'll bet that was a sight to behold," laughed Casey.

"YES! Covered and splattered in rainbow paint, you had a grand ol 'time."

It felt great to remember happy times mingled in with the sad.

The sunset, with vibrant pink and orange clouds, provided a glorious background for the end of an emotional day. A golden glow reflecting on the rippling waves had a spiritual, cleansing element.

"What a life you've led, Aunt Laurie," Casey said.

The two women embraced. Casey tried to absorb some of her aunt's pain, and Laurie tried to shield Casey from the trauma of her life.

The sangria was gone and they were utterly spent. It was understood that Laurie had reached her limit of talk for the time being. Her body language also let Casey know not to ask the burning questions in her mind.

A few days later they joined a group by the pool for a resort party and concert. Samples of rum drinks were being offered to the guests. Casey and Aunt Laurie didn't hesitate to try the refreshing beverages. As a matter of fact, they took one for each hand because it was encouraged by the servers. "Why not?" laughed Aunt Laurie.

"We're on vacation," Casey reminded her aunt.

They both wore colorful sundresses they bought from a beach vendor the day before. Since it was a party, they brought out their jewelry.

Casey's new moonstone pendant shone against her suntanned glow, the perfect addition to the short blue and green off-the-shoulder dress.

Laurie's dress was long and loose with a yellow and teal design. Her turquoise necklace and sparkling sterling dangle earrings added to her festive mood.

There was a crowd, but the two of them started out dancing alone.

The two women swayed happily, completely uninhibited. The dark rum and island breezes worked magic as they danced, worry-free.

Soon the area was alive with reggae music and other dancers joined them. The evening included more tropical drinks along with toasts, with everyone raising their glasses to each other's health and happiness.

"Tonight reminds me of a trip we took when I was a little girl," Casey said as they strolled back towards their cottage after the festivities of the evening.

"I'm amazed you remember that short vacation. You were only about six years old and we flew to Key West for a long weekend. You loved the music and danced then, too. I have pictures somewhere; you were adorable with your curls bouncing around in the wind. I recall eating at a seaside cafe and you tried key lime pie for the first time. Rather than super sweet, the pie had a tart kick to it. I was waiting for you to pucker up your face. Instead, you beamed with delight. Even the waitress was surprised how you gobbled it up and asked for a second slice!" she fondly reminisced.

"I still love key lime pie and yours is the absolute best!" Casey praised her aunt.

"The recipe I use is from Key West. Believe it or not, the waitress slipped the recipe to me when I paid the tab. They boasted it was the best in town, and I was told they rarely shared the recipe. Your powers of persuasion were developing even at age six, Casey," Laurie teased.

Shenanigans

Two days later, as they were packing, "I can't believe we have to leave this sweet cottage. We can take our suitcases to the front desk. Then we still have a few hours before we head to the airport. How do you want to spend the end of our trip?" Casey inquired.

Laurie absent-mindedly stuffed her wrinkled clothing in her suitcase, which had been tidily packed when they arrived. "What about checking out the hot tub? I'd love to soak these tired muscles from dancing the other night," she admitted. "That's probably the most exercise I've had in years."

"Sounds like an excellent plan," said Casey, doing a rhythmic happy dance.

Finishing up and about to haul the luggage

to the front desk, they surveyed the room, loving the white-washed walls and shabby chic decor. On the ceiling, a small crystal chandelier spread rays of sunny light across the room. The cottage was partially shaded by the lush fronds and they could smell fragrant tropical flowers from the open windows. The bungalow and tropical beach provided the ideal setting for their heart-to-heart conversations and fun-filled days.

Casey certainly learned more about her mom and their life in New York with Aunt Laurie. She couldn't help but wonder, *What about my dad?* An important question that was still a mystery.

When the two arrived at the hot tub it was occupied by only one woman. She smiled sweetly, her face flushed; obviously she'd been there for way too long. She exited shortly after, leaving them to relax in the secluded area surrounded by swaying palms.

Both women settled in, feeling grateful, allowing their legs to float, using some spare towels for softness beneath their heads. It was blissful.

"This is perfect, isn't it?" Aunt Laurie said in a dreamy voice. Casey replied in agreement with a nod. Both murmured a deep sigh of contentment and closed their eyes, "Ahhhhh." The slight movement of the trees whispered a breeze over their grateful hearts.

Five or ten minutes later, "Is that singing?" Casey asked. Their serenity was disturbed by off-key lyrics reminiscent of an Irish bar song. As the singing became louder, they realized they were about to be serenaded by a group of inebriated men.

"Oh, no," exclaimed Aunt Laurie. "I can't imagine this ending well."

"Ooh, Danny boy. Oh, Danny boy, I love you sooo," was upon them. The jovial men, oblivious they were in the company of others, sloshed their beverages and continued to belt out the tune.

"Leave this to me, Aunt Laurie. Just follow my lead," Casey whispered without a moment's hesitation.

Skeptical, Laurie flashed a reluctant smile.

Once the men realized they had stumbled upon the two women, chaos ensued. One slipped and nearly fell into the water. Another cleared his throat to make an announcement, but then looked around stupefied at a loss for words. The younger of the three turned red from embarrassment by the shenanigans. He sported an auburn beard and could have easily been mistaken for a leprechaun.

"You're drinking whiskey? Don't you know you're in rum country, gentleman," Casey said with authority and a gleam in her eye. She looked directly at the younger of the men, gave a flirty wink, and instructed, "Go get us a bottle of rum and we'll show you how it's done, island style." The befuddled and harmless men blinked back in confusion. "What are you waiting for?" Casey interrogated in her well-practiced courtroom voice.

All three clamored towards the bar on an important mission. From behind, they resembled unstable toddlers about to take an unfortunate nosedive on the concrete.

Aunt Laurie dried off. "What on earth are you thinking, Casey?" She had a look of total disbelief on her face.

"I'm thinking we get the hell out of here before they stumble back with more atrocious songs and realize they've been bamboozled," Casey blurted with a splash exiting the hot water.

Laurie fumbled to catch up, as Casey shouted, "Hurry, quick, RUN!"

Hold the Anchovies

One mild Saturday morning, Jacob and Sophie walked over to Sophie's cabin. Since their engagement, she'd decided to sell her cabin and property. "This is a special place and I loved it the moment I saw it," she said to Jacob, her new fiancé. "Since we will be neighbors, I don't want to sell to just anyone."

"We don't have to rush the sale. The perfect buyer will come along," he said encouragingly.

Sophie exhaled slowly and lovingly tightened the grip on his hand slightly, in agreement.

They were both falling in love with Jacob's renovated family house and it was becoming their home. Little by little, customized touches were added to personalize the shared homestead, inside and out.

Strolling, still hand in hand around the mostly drab winter landscape, Sophie knew putting the cabin on the market in the near future was the right decision. Hints of green sprouts peeked through the cold earth, promising spring was soon arriving. She had moved into the cabin after Sonya passed away, and the home with its natural environment helped her cope with the tragedy and rebuild her spirit, which was ready to move on to new beginnings now, too.

Sophie and Sonya went on a fabulous trip to Italy right before the global pandemic hit. The vacation included days of joyfully traipsing through the various Italian regions on adventures. They purchased from talented jewelry artists for their boutique, while sampling specialized food and wine from each Italian region. Laughter and dancing with total abandon, had created precious memories during that time.

After quite a delay, due to quarantines and slow delivery, Sophie received the boxes of jewelry she and Sonya purchased together. The boxes had stayed untouched and unopened in the basement of the cabin for a long time. Sophie was too distraught with emotions to even consider opening the jewelry without Sonya. Delving into the tissue-filled boxes of jewelry together for their boutique was like Christmas every time and never got old.

After a healing process, which was facilitated

by new friendships and the beauty of nature, Sophie was able to unwrap and appreciate the dazzling jewelry. Of course, by that time, the boutique they owned together was closed and long gone.

In a moment of compassion and clarity, Sophie realized that giving the new jewelry to wonderful friends was the closure she needed. One by one, close friends were invited to the cabin. Sophie, in remembrance of her dear sister, gave the precious gemstone jewelry as gifts to those who helped her through the most challenging of times.

"How are you feeling about your Twins Silver Dream Boutique becoming a pizza place?" Jacob asked Sophie as they headed towards the creek.

"Those years seem like a dream now. I have so many happy memories of us when we first opened the boutique. Sonya and I loved creating jewelry displays and seeing the smiles from customers discovering the perfect gemstones. If I recall correctly, you were one of those customers, my dear."

"I certainly was, and returning to Duck Creek was the best decision of my life," Jacob asserted.

Sophie responded, "If you hadn't visited the store that time to buy jewelry, I may not have had the gumption to contact you. I remembered you being kind, humble, and considerate. It just didn't add up to the craziness of selling your beautiful childhood home to a bunch of money-hungry businessmen."

Jacob affectionately caressed her ample der-
riere in reply.

Today was the friends and family soft re-
opening of Bryan's Cafe & Pizzeria. The renovations were complete and, luckily, they were able to
stay partially open during most of the construction phase. The regular customers in Duck Creek
had been understanding through the renovations,
excited about the upcoming change in the menu.

Bryan had been working on the details of the
day for weeks.

"I think we're ready. Thanks for your patience and dedication. You're a vital part of this
restaurant and I appreciate each of you," he honestly told the restaurant servers and other staff.

The previous year Paul, the landlord, had
agreed to the expansion of the cafe into the next-
door space, which had been empty since Twins Silver Dream closed down.

Now, the outside was adorned with brand
new bright red awnings, which could be seen
down the block. Black window boxes held fresh,
aromatic mini evergreens adding another dash of
color. The plan was to have a variety of seasonal
flowers and plants in the boxes year-round.

The large polished windows sparkled a warm

greeting to the waiting crowd. The expanded restaurant looked inviting and updated.

The rustic barn board sign was designed and hand-painted by a talented graphic designer and artist, Kay Fenton. The restaurant name was in a bold red script, with deep etched green and gold vines curled around the corners.

"I love the new sign," Sophie mentioned as they entered.

Jacob said, "The new awning and sign are welcoming, don't you think? I can tell the window boxes are handcrafted, too."

"Yes, and you would notice the craftsmanship," she replied with an amused glimmer in her eye.

Once inside, "Look at the amazing brick oven!" was heard over and over again as friends and family arrived for the opening. The new oven had a large curved arch, with the flames visible from most of the tables on that side of the new pizzeria.

Brian explained to a friendly group, "The pizza has a smoky flavor, and the toppings will be slightly crunchy due to the high temperature. Just wait until you taste it. This pizza will certainly surpass all other types you've tried," he boasted.

Just then, servers walked by with a selection

of pizza and other delicacies to sample.

Sophie and Jacob tasted everything. "We should go out to dinner in town more often," Jacob declared.

Sophie replied, "Let's plan a date next week. Maybe Amanda and Tony would like to join us."

His reaction was a broad smile and nod.

The wait-staff circulated with trays of wine, but there was also a horseshoe-shaped bar connecting the old and new sections of the cafe. The polished refurbished wood counter gleamed with seating for about a dozen people.

"The stools are nearly full," Jacob mentioned.

"Starting soon, we'll be open later some evenings and hope to have live music on weekends," Casey overheard Jeff, the newly hired publicist, say to a group enjoying a selection of artisan pizza samples.

Sipping a local pinot noir, Casey mingled with friends as Jeff walked over, dressed in a crisp, pink designer shirt with a logo she recognized as Gucci from a few of the pompous attorney contacts she knew. His hair was slicked back and she could smell his overpowering cologne as he approached. He stood within inches of her, invading her personal space.

He leaned in even closer and asked in a gravelly voice, "So, it's Casey right? Is it Ms., Miss, or Mrs.?"

The gender-marital identities happened to be one of her pet peeves.

Casey stood up taller in her heels and midnight blue wrap-around dress. She straightened her shoulders and took a step away from him, just as Noah entered the room and saw the brief encounter.

As Noah approached, Casey spoke in a clear voice and replied, "I don't understand why women are put into categories according to whether they are married or single. A man is always referred to as Mr. regardless of their relationships. It's just one more thing that demeans women in general."

As she turned to walk away without waiting for a response, there was Noah with a twinkle in his green eyes.

"My sister and mom have this same conversation frequently and I agree. In this day and age, why do we still use antiquated titles? My family can really get going on the topic of women's rights and inequalities. My sister has a long list of respected, historical women she can quote," Noah spoke with pride.

The last sentence went unheard, as Casey

looked into his smiling eyes. She remembered Noah from Thanksgiving but hadn't noticed his charming dimples.

The conversation switched over to art when she spotted a wonderful painting of a baby fawn displayed on the wall.

"Are you familiar with Molly's work?" Noah asked.

"No, but I love this painting and look at these baby chicks. They look so fluffy and real!"

Noah remarked, "Molly Sims is extremely talented. I carry her work at my store, along with other local artists. You might recognize the name Brenda Kidera? She's becoming very well-known and I also carry her remarkable work."

"Your store is the one where Amanda purchased all of those quirky birds?" Casey inquired.

"Yes, that's the one." He elaborated, "It feels so good for community members, like Bryan and his cafe, to support our local painters. I'd love for you to stop by sometime, Casey. I'll give you a personal tour and treat you to lunch afterward?"

"That sounds truly lovely, Noah." Casey smiled, oblivious that Amanda and Tony were peering through the crowd at them, making an effort to look nonchalant.

As they made their way towards Tommy and Leya, Noah pointed out another gorgeous painting, "This lake scene is by another artist named Stephanie Porta. Don't you love the way she captures the light?"

"Yes, it's beautiful. I wish I had more wall space in my little apartment," she admitted to Noah.

"Ah, congratulations!" Casey declared a minute later as Bryan affectionately put his arm around her. "Everything looks amazing. It's wonderful to see all your plans come to life."

"Thanks. You know I've been thinking about expanding for quite some time, and it's exciting to have it complete," Bryan shared.

Leya added with enthusiasm, "My favorite lunch spot will now become a date night destination with music."

"Maybe we can all meet for happy hour on Fridays," Noah suggested to the group.

Bryan smiled and shook his head, appreciative of the community support.

"I saw you admiring the paintings," Bryan said to Casey. "Did Noah tell you that a different artist will be featured every few months? So, if you see a painting you love, it's for sale. Most of the artists also have their work available at his store, The Treehouse."

Casey couldn't help but notice Noah beaming with pride as Bryan explained the featured artists and how the Treehouse was participating in the community support for local artists. *Oh, those dimples. I think I'll visit the art gallery sometime very soon.*

Fire-Breathing Dragon

Amanda was up in the middle of the night, for the umpteenth night in a row. She didn't know why, and she was beyond annoyed. She was chilly enough to add fuzzy socks with her winter pajamas before bedtime, then ended up tearing the socks off, along with her pajamas some nights and throwing off the blankets, sweating.

I'm hot, I'm cold, I can't sleep, she murmured to herself as she basically wandered around the house zombie-like. *It's 2 o'clock in the morning.*

Her mind was exhausted and jumping:

~ *Will my Christmas cactus bloom again?*
~ *Do I hear mice in the attic?*
~ *I'm going to make playdough for the church daycare.*
~ *Are we out of pickles?*

~ Am I depressed, or just grouchy because I can't sleep?

Amanda was experiencing serious mood swings and Tony wasn't sure what to do.

"I can't seem to do anything right these days," he finally said to her one morning at breakfast. "One day you appreciate my help with your on-line orders; the next day you are yelling at me for being in the way." He hesitated, but needed to get his feelings out in the open. "Should I just leave you alone? Do you want to hire an assistant?" he asked in a husky voice filled with frustration.

Amanda sat very still across the table from her loving husband and burst into tears. He got up and led her into the living room without saying a word. They sat on the couch while she cried, messy and loud. He quietly handed her tissues.

"I don't know what's wrong with me, Tony. My thoughts are all jumbled and I feel like crying all the time," she admitted.

Amanda wrung her hands together, trying to get a hold of her erratic emotions.

A few minutes later, she continued, "I feel like I've been hijacked. I have no control. I'm not sure how else to explain it."

Amanda took in a deep breath and released it slowly before she went on.

"My shoulders and jaw are tense all the time. I can't concentrate. My business is disorganized. I'm falling behind in all the accounting and orders. Plus, I'm not sleeping."

Tony was listening intently but not fully understanding, although he was trying.

"We go to bed at the same time together every night," he said with a puzzled expression.

"Yes, and I've been awake most nights for weeks now," Amanda hiccuped in between sobs.

"Maybe you should go see a doctor?" Tony said with reservation, as he knew she preferred natural treatments.

"I'm going into town for a haircut with Laurie this morning. I'll call the doctor's office for an appointment when I get home," Amanda answered weakly.

"Do you want to rest for a while?" he asked gently. "I can close the shades and put on your meditation music?" He hesitated, but added, "How about a shoulder massage?"

"No, I have too much to do and my hair appointment is at 10 a.m. I probably wouldn't be able to relax and sleep anyways," she answered with a defeated moan.

At that point, he understood that she needed

a few minutes alone, so he walked out on the porch, to give her some space.

When Amanda walked into Citrine she immediately noticed the pleasant updates. She saw new furniture in the waiting area and a few children were sitting together on a bean bag chair reading.

I miss reading to children. Maybe Casey will have children someday and I can read them stories. Casey and Noah could have babies with dimples and red curls. Oh, how sweet. What am I thinking? I don't even know if they're dating. I'm predicting the future like a crazy woman.

"Welcome," said Beverly, interrupting Amanda's daydream about curly-haired babies. "It's been quite a while since you were here, Amanda."

"Yes, it has. How have you been, Beverly?

"Very well, thanks for asking."

"What is the wonderful scent?" Amanda motioned her hands, wafting the aroma towards her face.

"It's a synergy-blended essential oil. It's helpful for relaxation and focus," responded Beverly pleasantly.

"Well, it's working. I suddenly feel more relaxed than I have in weeks."

Laurie walked over just then and gave her longtime friend a hug and invited her to come back to her styling station.

"It's been over a year, right?" asked Laurie.

Amanda answered quietly. "Yes, you know me well. My long gray hair doesn't get much attention."

Laurie laughed and pointed to her own head, "You mean like me? I prefer the description silver, though. It sounds more sophisticated than gray."

Her friend's hair was peppered with silver highlights and piled in a messy bun, the ends sticking out in every direction.

"At least you didn't start going gray in your thirties as I did," stated Amanda.

"I could have colored it for you anytime you wanted," Laurie reminded her.

The two women had grown close years ago when Laurie moved into the house next to Amanda. It was back when Casey was just a little girl and Amanda was a school teacher.

"I heard all about Casey and her yoga classes," said Laurie. "She's really excited about teaching with the baby goats at Chestnut Hill."

"I was hoping I wasn't being too bossy in suggesting she become a yoga instructor," responded Amanda. "She was a natural during the classes, and I could just imagine her teaching."

As Amanda sat in her dear friend's chair with her hair loose and wet, she physically felt her shoulders soften and her jaw release.

"Are we doing the regular trim?"

"I wish you would perform your magic to help me sleep and unjumble my brain," Amanda said with a frown.

"Hmmm, unjumble your brain, huh?" she said, placing her index finger on her chin in thought.

"Are you also burning hot and freezing cold within a few minutes of each other? Do you have irrational, rambling thoughts that come from nowhere?"

Amanda popped her eyes wider when Laurie added, "Do you feel like crying for no reason?"

Amanda looked up into the mirror and saw her friend smiling.

"How in the world did you know?"

"Welcome to your journey through menopause!" Laurie declared with a wave of her hand

and a dramatic bow. She pretended to fan herself with both hands as she looked at her friend's surprised expression.

"Menopause? My, my, I thought I was finished. I had hot flashes several years ago, and my cycle has nearly stopped."

"That was probably the beginning of perimenopause. The symptoms can change, evolve, and last for years," her friend enlightened.

Amanda was caught off guard and just sat there confused. *Menopause?*

Laurie told Amanda, "Beverly gave me some herbs, aromatherapy, and other holistic remedies, and my symptoms are now hardly noticeable. I mean, I'm still tired from standing most days and get occasional flashes, but I'm finally in control of my emotions, and boy, was I a hot mess!"

Laurie recalled, "We had an accountant come to the salon to assist with taxes a couple of years ago. We were closed and I was the only one here." She paused to chuckle at the memory. "He was on the computer at the reception desk and I was sitting on the couch with my iPad. The hot flash came welling up from the core of my being like an inferno, and you know, they aren't exactly short flashes. The flames of the beast last way longer than a flash. Anyway, I blurted out, 'power surge' aloud, instead of in my head. He ran over to me thinking it was a technical issue. I had to explain, while sweating profusely and fanning myself with a magazine, that I was having a hot flash."

Amanda smiled a silly grin when she realized she wasn't going bat shit crazy. She relaxed into her chair, pleased and extremely relieved her friend could relate to her on all levels of this life change.

Beverly listened to their conversation from across the room with a gracious smile. "I am happy to recommend a few things I think will help," she said, walking over to join the ladies.

Amanda said, "The essential oils you have in the diffuser would be a great start. I can't believe how much better I felt after just a couple of minutes."

While Beverly went to answer the phone, Amanda thought *poor Tony* and began laughing uncontrollably.

"What's so funny about menopause?" her friend wanted to know.

"I had a little breakdown of sorts this morning with Tony. I almost called him a fire-breathing dragon!"

"What? Please, tell me more. Ha! This should be good."

"Well, at night I can't sleep. I lay there wide awake for hours, thinking crazy thoughts. He's sound asleep next to me like always, but his breath feels so hot...I swear, one night I saw him as a fire-breathing dragon."

They both started giggling. It was truly the best Amanda had felt in ages.

"And, I think I came very close to smacking him in the head with my pillow."

"Oh, Lordy," Laurie blurted. "This life change will eventually be a happy destination. I promise. There's freedom in becoming older, and also in realizing what's going on with your body during this time," declared her wise friend.

Amanda left feeling lighter with an overall sense of calm. Her beautiful hair shone smooth and toned and in a long side braid. She carried a list of items available at the shop nearby, thanks to Beverly.

Before walking to Sage and Thyme to pick up her arsenal of menopause remedies, she sent a quick text to Tony.

"Hi, honey. All is well. I'll explain everything when I get home. I love you so much. P.S. I'm not going crazy after all. XXOO"

Buttercup

"Good afternoon, Amanda, I see we have a few new kids! Who's this little adorable fluff ball?" asked Casey.

"Meet Buttercup. Isn't she the cutest baby ever?" replied Amanda. Gesturing to the other side of the goat enclosure, she added, "And over there, we have Marigold and her brother Memphis. The twins are hard to tell apart, with nearly the same black and white markings. I've noticed Marigold is friendlier and enjoys attention. Memphis keeps to himself and runs away when approached. Let's see if it's true during the yoga session today."

Tony agreed with his wife about the twins and joined them in the goat pen, as Casey smiled and gave Buttercup an affectionate rub behind the ears. "Ooh, you like this," she murmured to the little goat as Buttercup burrowed in for more and responded with a tiny bleat of approval, causing two more baby goats to come skipping over.

"We call this brown baby Acorn, and the little one trying to jump on his back is Hazel," laughed Tony. "Oh, believe me, this crew will keep you busy today."

Casey responded, "I looked at the list, and we have about a dozen participants this afternoon." Glancing around she said, "I think we have more goats than people."

Amanda said, "Clare and her youngest daughter, Annie, will be joining the class. Renee is off for a riding lesson with Connie today. Clare gets a special day with Annie."

"Having little Annie here will be really fun," Casey declared."It looks like the class will be all ages today. Remember a few weeks ago when we had the girl scout troop? Boy, I've never heard so much laughter. The goats were extremely jovial that day. The troop leader emailed later and said the girls 'faces were sore from so much giggling and smiling. They want to come back again."

Amanda said, "Great," and remarked, "I have a few small bowls of shredded carrots ready for the helpers. The snack really encouraged the baby goats to interact with the scouts during that class, as I recall. We know everyone wants attention from our babies!"

The guests started to arrive and claim their spots, and soon the colorful yoga mats were scattered around the open field with spaces in between for the baby goats to romp. Some people sported color-coordinated yoga outfits that looked to be brand new, while others had on casual shorts and tee shirts.

"Hi, Stacey and Sam," Casey greeted her neighbors from her apartment house. "Come on over here and let me introduce Jayne and Mary, the interns from work."

"It's wonderful to meet you," they greeted each other and unrolled their mats in preparation.

"This is Marigold and Buttercup," Casey said, as the little goats jumped over the mats and bumped into their legs playfully.

"This is going to be so fun!" said Stacey, as she pulled her wavy blonde hair in a ponytail.

"I can't decide which one is going to be my new BFF," announced Sam. Just then, Marigold burped in response.

The friends all laughed, and Stacey said, "Sam, meet your new bestie."

Casey walked over to set up the music to play a selection of Native American-style flute by musician B.Gall. She was introduced to the music recently and found it enchanting and ideal for yoga practice.

After quieting the group with a few taps of her triangle, Casey began, "Welcome to Yoga with Baby Goats at Chestnut Hill Farm. Just relax and have a good time. There's no judgement here, and especially no right or wrong way to participate. The goal is simply to enjoy this peaceful farm setting and let the cuteness overload of the goats calm your mind," explained Casey.

A hand in the back shot up with the question, "Will the goats climb on us?"

"Great question," Casey replied. "It's hard to predict what they'll do," she said with a laugh. The babies are between two and six months old and weigh no more than 25 pounds. You'll see that Amanda and Tony have given each goat a collar labeled with their names. It's typical for them to frolic and nuzzle you for attention. It's up to you how much you want to play with our kid friends," Casey held the complete attention of the participants. "However, the plank, tabletop, and child poses seem to be their favorite, since they have easier access for climbing. Also, It's a fact they'll literally eat anything. Please keep all personal belongings tucked away in your bags to keep the babies safe," she added.

Some skeptical and nervous giggling chirped

through the group, but most were eager to get started.

The goats scattered among the area, happily exploring and checking out new willing friends. The group laughed and excitedly started talking, while Casey worked to get the class's attention back to start the session.

"Let's stand at the top of our mats with our feet grounded. Make an effort for every inch of your sole to touch your mat, even each of your toes. Yoga is about being present in the moment and honoring our minds and bodies." She looked over the crowd and smiled, "Take in a deep breath, open your chest and lift your face towards the sun." Observing the group and hesitating for each to truly participate, she continued, "Now, release intentionally to my count, one, two, three, four. Let's spread our arms and lift them to the sky, take in another breath, and exhale to my count."

Meanwhile, Annie started giggling, "Poppy is sniffing my butt and trying to eat my shirt!"

Clare, her Mom, knelt down adjusting her phone, laughing as she snapped a picture of Annie. While still on one knee, the adorable little cinnamon-colored baby stumbled and nuzzled her belly for a snuggle, and Clare couldn't resist. "You are a little sweetheart," she declared to her new friend.

The goats were comfortable and happy to

hop around from person to person. A few laughing ladies abandoned all hope of performing the poses, and just sat crossed legged on the ground with the goats vying for attention. They were a magnet for the critters to wander aimlessly, attempt to gnaw their hair, and nibble daintily at brightly colored painted toes, with no concept of personal space.

The bleating and burping sounds, *maaaa, baaaa,* and a few *erpks* were allowing the crowd to relax even more so, and unrestrained belly laughs blended with the goat noises.

Amanda stated to no one in particular as she wandered around, "I can't wait to see all these pictures."

Annie ran by, holding onto her "Girls Rule" shirt in a bunch around her waist. A tiny goat named Mozart jumped close by nipping and furtively trying in vain to snack on the bright orange tee. Annie giggled as she stated, "Oh no you don't, Mr. Mo. You're not getting my favorite shirt!"

Baby Hazel's chin dribbled from a quick drink from a bowl of water. Jayne exclaimed, "Well, thanks! I needed that cool refreshing break," as she swiped her hand across her dripping cheek, after Hazel got close and personal.

Her friend Mary just shook her head, and muttered, "Better you than me."

Casey viewed the scene from the sideline and

smiled. The amazing support from her neighbors and dear friends suddenly hit her. A warm rush of gratitude overwhelmed her thoughts.

After going through all the poses and sharing the final "Namaste" with the group, she knew each session would be fulfilling, funny, and worthwhile. She loved yoga and the baby goats made it so interesting and hysterically special.

"Thanks so much!" said a group of young girls as they headed out across the field, "We can't wait to sign up for more classes!"

The crowd was thinning out, and Sam, Stacey, and Casey sat under the big chestnut tree with the rolled-up mats discarded off to the side, like oversized fruit roll-ups.

"You are a master yoga teacher! Your passion shines through the chaos of the energetic baby goats," said Sam, as the neighbors enjoyed some iced tea Amanda had just delivered.

"I'm glad you were here today, Sam. Seeing you grounded me and made me appreciate the goodness of the day."

Sam smiled with a shy nod and replied, "It was honestly the best yoga session I've ever attended with four-legged friends."

Stacey added, "You were in your element, Casey, and I can see why you love it out here so much. It's peaceful."

Moonbeams

"You remember that old oak tree in my back-yard when we were neighbors, don't you, Casey?" Amanda asked, with an affectionate tone.

The two women sat under the chestnut tree reminiscing long after the yoga guests had departed. The sun glowed against the horizon. It was still cool enough for sweaters.

"Yes, you called him Willie," Casey replied. "I know you used to sit under that tree all the time. I could see you hanging out there from my bedroom window when I was a little girl."

Amanda enlightened, "I haven't shared the details with many, but Willie was much more than an ancient oak tree. When I needed guidance, I would sit and meditate with my back relaxed against his trunk. Believe it or not, as I set intentions, and desires for answers to my circumstances he provided them."

"So, what exactly do you mean? The oak tree spoke to you?" Casey queried.

Amanda's smile was bright and filled with compassion. Casey focused on every word with interest as Amanda spoke.

"Anytime I felt the heaviness of the world and I needed wisdom, especially during the pandemic, I visited Willie the old oak that was my dear friend at the time. I leaned into him, closed my eyes, and waited," Amanda explained.

"And, what happened? What were you waiting for, exactly?" Casey questioned with childlike anticipation.

Amanda appreciated Casey's curiosity and responded, "Willie took me on adventures. I went into a trance-like state of mind. Sort of like savasana, when we rest at the end of the yoga session. Only it felt as if I were a participant in a movie being directed by Willie. Time was nonexistent during these hypnotic adventures. When it was over, I always received a life-changing message."

The two women, although a few decades apart in age, sat silently with the strong bond of life-long friends. The moonbeams broke through the tree line overhead, while the light danced between the branches creating speckles of silver on the ground.

"You can experiment with this chestnut tree, Casey," Amanda broke through the silence with encouragement. "Simply set an intention to receive what you need. There's nothing required of you but an open mind and heart." She reflected, "Ever since I moved to Chestnut Hill, I've felt this tree's magical vibes. Stay as long as you wish, my dear. It's cooling off and I'm turning in for the evening," Amanda said as she gave Casey an affectionate embrace and headed towards the farmhouse, disappearing past the sunflower field.

Skeptical and nervous, yet open, Casey adjusted her body to fit against the sturdy trunk of the chestnut tree. She gazed up at the deepening indigo twilight sky and said aloud, "I'm calling upon the wisdom of this night and to this magnificent tree to direct my thoughts for my highest good." Adding, "And so shall it be," in reassurance before closing her eyes.

The faint noises of the evening faded into the distance and Casey relaxed.

Exquisitely comfortable, she found herself peering at a beautifully detailed painting.

It was a portrait of a woman who seemed vaguely familiar, an artist from Mexico, Frida. Casey stared at the canvas, a colorful self-por-

trait, mesmerized by the marigolds woven in her hair and the embroidered dress she wore. Frida's shoulders glistened in the painting and the expression told secrets of lovers and passion unmatched by anyone Casey had ever known.

A conversation like a song vibrated in Casey's ears, in her mind, all the way down through her body.

The woman in the painting sang of dignity, truth, and feminism that Casey comprehended to her core. Years of torment wove a tapestry in her song, emphasized by the deep sorrow in her dark eyes. She sang the words directly to the confused young woman, and the timbre of her voice touched Casey's heart.

Your life is love.
You are the flowers, the trees, the stars.
Every moment is yours.
Live on your terms.
There are no regrets, just choices.
Make love and let it become your colorful mural.
Make love often.
Commit to your lover.
Your love is your art.

Casey opened her eyes, blinking, and noticing warmth despite the coolness of the evening. The temperature had dropped and the full moon glowed a ghostly orb of frosted light. The warmth touched her cheeks like a fever.

She gathered her yoga supplies, still mesmerized by the experience, moving to her car while reflecting upon the midnight hour and what had transpired under the chestnut tree. Casey vowed to share the fascinating details with Amanda someday in the near future.

Later that night, Casey dreamt of Frida's message. It all became as crystal clear as the moonbeams on that transformative evening.

The Log Cabin

"Sophie, I'm amazed you've cleared out the cabin so quickly and I'm appreciative that you even had it professionally cleaned," Casey gushed, carrying a box up the steps as Sophie held the door for her.

Sophie smiled and responded, "Jacob and I are beyond thrilled that you're our new neighbor. Negotiations were simple, and with your legal knowledge, the settlement was quick and smooth."

Moving day included a few friends and a warm meal of roasted herbed chicken and buttery mashed potatoes along with a scrumptious chocolate cake provided by Amanda.

"Amanda, the cake is amazing, and you know how my sweet tooth hasn't changed since childhood. Is this the same recipe you used when we were neighbors in town when I was a little girl? Casey inquired.

"It sure is and I'm happy to share it with you. Now that you're a homeowner, and have this spacious kitchen, you'll probably be baking more," Amanda replied.

"Thanks. Yes, I'm committed to becoming a little more domestic in this cozy cabin in the woods," Casey said as Aunt Laurie placed her arm around her waist.

"By the way, Amanda, Casey made your cinnamon buns for me and she's mastered your recipe! You'd be proud of her." Laurie shared.

"Wait, what?" Sam said playfully as she came around the corner. "You can bake, Casey? I'm learning more and more about you everyday." Casey just grinned and handed Sam a slice of cake.

A few days later Casey said with gratitude, "Noah, I loved visiting your gallery. I certainly didn't expect you to deliver the paintings personally. I can't thank you enough." Noah lifted the large snowy owl painting out of his truck and brought it into the front door with expert care.

Casey noticed Noah's wide shoulders as she followed him into her brand new home. *I bet he can hold a plank pose.* Casey's mind wandered to her yoga classes for a brief moment. Her favorite student, Sam, had recently seized a plank pose for a record amount of time, her compact frame giving her astonishing strength and balance.

"No problem, Casey. When we were at Bryan's for happy hour, I could see how excited you were when sharing your plans about moving into Sophie's cabin. I knew these wildlife paintings by Molly would perfectly suit the setting. The sweet little duck painting by Brenda is just adorable, like you Casey. We should meet at the cafe again soon. Your crazy goat stories are hilarious."

He returned from his truck a second time with an oil painting featuring playful baby cubs. "The whimsical nature of these little guys will make you smile everyday," Noah promised as he leaned the framed masterpiece against the wall by the stairs.

"I appreciate your guidance with my purchases and that you've spent so much time with me lately, Noah. Your help with moving my furniture, and now with decorations, has been invaluable," Casey said with genuine affection. "I'm thankful beyond words," she finished.

With a radiant smile, Noah waved goodbye and headed back to his truck. Once settled behind the wheel he glanced in the rear view mirror hoping to catch another glimpse of her auburn curls. Casey was a wonderful young woman. He admired her tenacity. Noah enjoyed being with her, whether it was at the gallery or hauling furniture to her new cabin. *I'm looking forward to spending more time together.*

On the way home, Noah's mind focused on Casey and her new home. The cabin in the woods was a perfect setting. It was close to town, yet quiet and peaceful near Duck Creek, plus there were neighbors whom she could rely on. His thoughts bounced around like a firefly in the summer as he drove down the winding country road.

He had noticed her front step railing was loose. Maybe he could bring some tools and tighten it up on his next visit. Although she was an independent young woman, Noah found his mind in an unfamiliar protective mode.

~ *The front porch could use work. It wouldn't be complicated to enlarge it while doing repairs. It's a perfect setting for star-gazing.*

~ *The pile of wood would make more sense if moved closer to the door.*

~ *More lights for winter evenings, it's dark back in the woods.*

Noah was still smiling the following morning as his phone *dinged*. "I hung the paintings and they are perfect. Thanks again," Casey texted.

"Maybe I'll swing by in a few days and take a look," he replied.

Casey sent a little owl emoji as an answer.

As the day wore on, Noah considered possible projects related to the log cabin, now owned by a certain nature-loving yoga instructor.

It's beginning to feel like a home, Casey thought as she sat with her coffee a few days later, admiring the beauty of her newly acquired art. Such detail and life-like critters displayed on her walls. The astonishing part, a peek out of her windows and she could observe forest animals in their natural habitat. This home was a dream come true. *I am a tree-hugging country girl.*

Within a few months, the events leading to the purchase of the log cabin had unfolded in perfect harmony. Divine intervention is what Sam had called it. "There's no need to question when the Universe hands you a beautiful gift," Sam explained mindfully.

Sam and Casey had been neighbors, sharing a wall in an apartment situated in a renovated house in Oak Glen. Through the course of getting to know one another, it was discovered they both had a soft spot for animals, especially those who required extra tender loving care.

"This sweet little dog rescued me today," Casey had said to her neighbor one evening after walking the tiny pomeranian called Elvis. He was her latest in a series of recent adoptions. "The poor fellow was neglected but now he's going to live out his retirement years with me in luxury."

Sam nodded in agreement with a look of understanding. "My playful kitties, Ralph and Rosie, are starting to acclimate to their *furever* home, finally," said Sam. "It took them a while to realize they're safe now. I'm glad that the shelter owner, Freya, encouraged me to rescue them as a pair," she said as the two calico kittens rolled off the couch tangled in a clumsy ball. "And, Kevin, my rambunctious terrier, has taken them under his wing as if it's his personal duty to protect his furry siblings," Sam reported with a bit of pride.

Casey observed with appreciation, "Lucy, my laid-back beagle, doesn't know what to think about the growing family. She just takes it all in stride."

The two women had been spending many evenings together as their friendship blossomed. All of the animals were frequently gathered in one of their apartments. "It looks like we're running an animal shelter," they often joked.

A talented musician, Sam had a unique way of calming the pets down with impromptu songs. The posse of animals, snuggled in a heap, would end up sleeping soundly with just a few melodies. It had become an evening ritual. Strumming a guitar and sharing songs, Sam showered each animal with harmonic love until purring and snoring could be heard from every corner of the apartment. Casey watched with amazement.

Sam's mother had recently shared, "When she was just a toddler, she sang before she talked."

They would have been perfectly content continuing to share a wall in the apartment building, yet the universe had much different plans.

The formal letter had come as an unwelcome shock.

> *Residents,*
>
> *It has come to our attention that the policy of no pets in the Parkside House Apartments has been violated. Due to this situation, each violating tenant has thirty days to re-home their pets or vacate the premises. Kindly respond with your preference immediately.*
>
> *Regards, Smith Brothers Realtors*

The thirty days had been a whirlwind of packing, caring for the clan of animals, and precious moments of unbelievable patience.

Aunt Laurie supplied new luxurious linens and enough scented candles to last a lifetime. Beverly managed to create an oasis as she arranged their combined belongings in each of the rooms, utilizing her feng shui principles for the positive flow of energy.

Sophie stocked the kitchen cabinets and

fridge, left piles of firewood, curtains, and some furniture to make the first days of unpacking effortless. "I'm so grateful, Sophie. You're going to be the best neighbor ever. I hope you'll drop by to walk the labyrinth often," Casey encouraged as she hung up the phone.

Magical Moments

Casey watched through the window, she saw snow had begun to fall. In a short period of time, the ground was covered and darkness had set in. The gaggle of pets was snuggled safely with full bellies, in a variety of corners and soft beds. It appeared as if they'd lived in the cabin for years.

Casey lit a blazing fire in the stone fireplace and admired her handiwork as she added a few gleaming candles to the room. *Thanks, Aunt Laurie.*

The room was romantic and sublime. Sam will be home any minute. Casey felt a flutter of joy and expectation.

Entering their home, leaving her wet coat and boots at the door, Sam noticed the glorious warmth of the fire and gave Casey a flirtatious wink. "It's turning into a blizzard. Looks like we'll be snowed in for a few days," Sam sang.

"Samantha, my love. Welcome home," Casey whispered with outstretched arms.

Wrapped in an embrace, Samantha and Casey watched the quiet snow as the incandescent flames danced on the walls. It was the beginning of an exquisite life together that both women knew was surely magical.

Casey's Resources

*Beverly's Remedies for Symptoms of Menopause**

Black Cohosh Supplement: Created with the root of the North American black cohosh plant. Known to reduce hot flashes.

Meditation: Calming stress through meditation may help subdue random thoughts and create a grounding effect.

Flaxseed: Good source of lignans, which tend to balance female hormones. Eases night sweats in some women. Mix into cereals or bread dough before baking.

Peppermint oil: Place on the bottom of your feet before bed. Enjoy the cooling system effect.

Dark and Stormy Cocktail Recipe

Ingredients:

2 1/2 oz. dark Gosling's Black Seal rum
3 oz. ginger beer
Splash of lime juice (optional)
Lime wedges
Directions:

Fill a tall glass or copper mug with ice cubes. Add ginger beer.

Top with Gosling Black Seal rum and optional lime juice. It resembles a storm cloud and can be left or stirred.

Garnish with a lime wedge. Enjoy!

Casey's New Moon Ritual*

Start with a pad of paper and a pencil. Post-it notes work perfectly.

Write down what you wish to release or change in your life on each small piece of paper. Keep it basic and realistic.

Examples:

I release worries and thoughts concerning what others think of me.

I allow myself to say no without giving an explanation.

I will increase my yoga practice to a daily ritual.

Light a fire. Outside is best, when possible.

Toss some dried white sage into the flames for cleansing.

Take a few deep breaths as you let your gaze soften, using the flames to bring you into a serene state of mind.

Sit quietly for a few moments, simply focusing on the gentle beat of your heart. Let this be a special time of slowing down. Take as long as you need.

Toss the notes in the fire one by one.

For each, close your eyes and visualize your life changing. As you connect with the energy of the new moon, honor how your body and mind are feeling. See your intentions becoming your reality.

As you gain clarity, reflect upon your gratitude.

Casey's Animal Rescue Notes

I believe it's our moral responsibility to have compassion for all living creatures. Rescuing animals builds a community where people value and respect the lives of pets. In most cases, the joy of bringing home an animal that needs loving care improves our lives just as much as the new friend. I encourage you to consider adoption and animal rescue where you live. I'm convinced the decision will be a heart-warming experience.

Beverly and Casey are fictional characters in this story. Information not intended as medical advice, diagnosis or treatment for symptoms or conditions. Consult your physician before considering holistic treatments.

Communicate with the authors, Patti Sapp and Susan Lavin on social media: Twins, Trees and Books.

Books In This Series

Tree Hugger Series

The Tree-Hugger Series features characters who utilize the beauty of nature. The fascinating manner in which trees facilitate healing and growth will astound the reader. After experiencing the series, you will be compelled to hug your favorite tree.

Listen To The Trees

Listen to the Trees Listen to the Trees is Book 1 of the Tree Hugger Series.

Amanda is a visionary. She's a risk-taker. Her friends admire her for her adventurous spirit. What happens when Amanda is faced with unexpected pandemic fears? With the support of mystical hypnotic opportunities, she manages to transform the fears into opportunities. Read to discover how she creates a second chance for love. Don't be suprised, also, if you suddenly have insatiable cravings for ice cream. It's a love story with metaphysical twists. A must-read for tree huggers who have a true appreciation for our natural world.

Magical Forest Musings

Magical Forest Musings Magical Forest Musings is Book 2 of the Tree Hugger Series.

Magical Forest Musings is a story of hope. The story features twin sister entrepreneurs, who live in a quaint town. The serenity of nature, intuition from an earth angel, and sharing kindness are catalysts to healing. There's an element of surprise that includes cupcakes, romance, and an unexpected gift.

Thank You

Thanks to all our wonderful readers who have left positive reviews. If you haven't done so and are willing, your support means to the world to us. - Susan and Patti

Praise For Author

The Tree-Hugger series speaks to the heart and brings the reader into the transformative world of nature. With true friendships, magical crystals, and epicurean delights to tempt the staunchest of dieters, the reader is whisked away to a world we all dream about in our souls. You will be pleasantly enchanted by The Tree-Hugger Series. Perfect reading material for a winter's day by the fire, or a lazy summer's afteroon in a sun-drenched hammack.

- PATTIE HOLY ILENDA (AMAZON REVIEW)